Tully knew there was no way out

"Very well, Mr. Meachem," she said defiantly. "I'll come with you since I appear to have no choice in the matter. But I'll tell you one thing for sure—your family will be left in no doubt whatsoever that I loathe, hate and detest the very sight of you."

Her feet barely touched the ground as Yate yanked her up against his body. His look was barbaric and if she had any doubts that he held all the high cards, he didn't leave her in doubt for very long.

"You say one word out of place when we get there," he threatened, "and I'll have you and that precious brother of yours behind bars so fast you won't have time to wonder what hit you!"

Hostage to Dishonour

by

JESSICA STEELE

Harlequin Books

TORONTO•LONDON•NEW YORK•AMSTERDAM
SYDNEY•HAMBURG•PARIS•STOCKHOLM

Original hardcover edition published in 1979
by Mills & Boon Limited

ISBN 0-373-02352-9

Harlequin edition published August 1980

Printed in U.S.A.

CHAPTER ONE

EVERYTHING in the garden, Tully thought with a sigh of satisfaction, was for once, lovely. Her brother Richard had come home from Meachem's in one of the brightest moods she had seen him in for a long time. Bright mood, she reflected happily, was perhaps an understatement for the high-spirited way he had breezed through the door of their apartment tonight. There had been an air of excitement about him, but knowing how quickly he could change from being happy and gay to being miserable and, it had to be faced, downright sulky, she had known better than to question him.

Perhaps he had a new girl-friend, she mused, as she strained the potatoes for their evening meal. Oh well, he would tell her in his own good time. Her thoughts left her brother and winged to the only other man in her life who could play havoc with her feelings—Howard, dear, wonderful Howard. Tully experienced again the flutterings of excitement whenever she thought of him. Richard, she knew, thought him stuffy, but then Richard didn't know Howard as she did.

The sound of the outer door opening, her brother's voice, still with that note of excitement in it, calling to her, 'I'm back!' had her turning her attention back to the potatoes; she'd been away there for a moment.

'Did you get it?'

Richard joined her in the kitchen holding aloft the bottle of Château de l'Abbaye they were going to have with their lamb chops. A rather grand gesture, she thought, particularly as Richard was always, but always, broke. But since he fancied himself as a wine connoisseur, and was so

happy about whatever little secret he must, she had decided, be nursing, she hadn't the heart to tell him his
money would be better spent in taking his shoes to be re-
paired. There had always been wine on the table in the
old days—but she wouldn't think about that.

'You'll be glad to see Monday, I expect,' Tully said con-
versationally when they were sitting down to their meal,
passing her wine glass over to Richard so that he could do
the honours.

'Monday, why?' he asked sharply, and had she not
known him better Tully would have thought his question
was one of aggressive guilt.

'Why, because Mr Burgess will be back then, won't he?'
she said quickly, hoping to forestall her brother's mood
changing to a fit of sulks if he had read her question as
meaning she thought he wasn't up to coping with the work
with the chief cashier away. 'It must be a strain doing his
job as well as your own—that's all I meant,' she said
placatingly.

'Oh yes—yes, I see what you mean.' Thank heaven he
was smiling again. She was going with Howard to meet his
parents tomorrow—a whole week more or less solely in his
company—and she wanted her holiday to be free from
worry about Richard and his peculiar moods of late.
'Actually I'm coping very well,' Richard said, and because
he was her brother the fact that his manner was somewhat
boastful went unnoticed. 'I can do old Burgess's job and
mine with both hands tied behind my back,' he declared,
and didn't look one bit abashed at his sister's look that
said she thought he might be just slightly overdoing it.

'He'll be retiring soon, won't he?'

'Not soon enough for my liking,' Richard stated, and
following Tully's line of thought, 'If you think I'm hanging
around on the offchance that they'll promote me in his
place you've got another think coming. I'm not waiting
five years only to be told I'm too young for the post.'

'But you'll be thirty by then. And you've said yourself how much they think of you. You've done so well in the two years you've been there and ...'

'Forget it, Tully,' Richard broke in. 'A lot of things can happen between now and then.' His eyes, dark brown like hers, took on a secretive look and she knew he had momentarily gone away from her. She knew of course that his heart had been set on going into the vine-growing and wine-making business, but that just wasn't possible any more.

'What sort of things can happen?' she asked tentatively, more to bring him back from chasing dreams that could never be realised than for any other reason.

'What?' Richard hadn't heard her question.

'I was asking what you envisage might happen in the next five years?'

'Well—lots of things,' Richard said vaguely. 'Old Burgess might decide not to retire. Retirement's not compulsory at Meachem's. The kingpin has a bee in his bonnet about nobody being put out to grass if they are fit and want to carry on.'

Tully well knew that Richard's slighting reference to the king-pin meant he was talking about Yate Meachem, the head of the Meachem Organisation. She had an idea that Richard had at some time over the past two years had a brush with Mr Meachem, and she wished Richard could forget his arrogance once in a while and remember they were no longer in a position where he could tell Mr Meachem what to do with his job. She sighed, forgetting completely that when the occasion demanded it she had been known to be a little haughty herself.

'Stop worrying about me,' said Richard. 'I'm well able to take care of myself, don't fret.' Again that secretive look came over his face, and thinking perhaps she might venture having her head snapped off if she asked him what had happened to make him so perky, Tully's thoughts were taken out of her head to hear him say, 'Anyway, you'll have enough to worry about without bothering your head about me.'

'What do you mean?'

'Well, you're all set to marry that stuffed shirt Howard Pearson, aren't you? It's tomorrow you're going to meet Mummy and Daddy, isn't it?'

'Howard is not a stuffed shirt,' Tully defended, getting hot under the collar when she had told herself time and time again she wouldn't every time Richard riled her on the same point. 'We're driving to Scotland in the morning,' she said more carefully. 'The fridge is full with everything you can possibly need, you'll only have to buy things like bread, the milkman will leave you a pint every day.'

'What time are you going?'

'Eight, Howard said—we've a long way to go, so he wants to make an early start.'

'So unless I get up with a lark I shan't see you again?'

'Well, not until a week on Sunday, but there's no need to get up, Richard, I know you like a lie in on Saturdays. I'll pop my head round your door before I go.'

'You've decided to marry him?' Richard asked, serious all at once.

Tully smiled back. Of late all Richard had been able to offer at the mention of Howard's name had been jeers, as though he thought Howard wasn't good enough for her. But it was nice to see him showing some real brotherly concern.

'Howard hasn't actually asked me yet,' she replied, knowing in her heart of hearts since he had dropped more than a hint or two, had told her he loved her and had confided that he had never taken a girl to meet his parents before, that he was serious about her.

'Waiting to see if Mummy and Daddy approve first, is he?'

'Richard!' said Tully warningly, and was surprised when he apologised at once.

'Sorry, Tully, that was a rotten thing to say. But seriously, do you want to marry him?'

Tully didn't have to think about it. 'Yes, I do,' she said quietly. 'I know you two don't quite hit it off, but yes, I want to marry him.'

Strangely, for all Richard's mocking, she thought he looked relieved at her answer. 'Well, you're old enough to know your own mind,' he said. 'You've had the vote for four years, so if he's the one you've elected to be *the* one, far be it from me to interfere. Though it's a wonder he hasn't snapped you up before now. I expect by the time you come back it will all be over bar the shouting—he's going to propose over the holiday, is he?'

It hadn't seemed quite right to have discussed Howard's intentions the way they had, Tully thought as she tackled the washing up while Richard went out for cigarettes he had forgotten when he'd gone for the wine. But at one time she and Richard had been very close, and she had felt close to him again as during their meal he had seemed, instead of opposing Howard as a future brother-in-law, now to come round to not only accepting the idea, but going as far as to say he was sure Howard would look after her, and that he, Richard, would not have to worry about her any more.

Tully had to smile as she hung the tea-towel to dry, running her eyes over the kitchen to check that everything was in place. The next time Richard worried about her would be the first. For all he was older by three years, it had been she who had been the one to look after him. She had learned very early on that given his head Richard invariably ended up in terrible trouble.

It hadn't always been like that, she reflected. Up until the time she was twelve she had always been his shadow.

Richard could do no wrong in her eyes then, or in her mother's eyes either, and between them they had spoiled him dreadfully. Then everything had changed. Mother had married Monty, and the spoiling Richard had been used to from her had dwindled. Oh, she had still loved him, had loved them all—her mother had had a great capacity for loving people, but once married to Monty, it was obvious that he had the greatest share of her love. Richard had been bewildered at first, then in an effort to take his mother's attention from Monty, had got himself into one scrape after another, and after one particularly outrageous prank, when it had taken weeks for the dust to settle, Tully had made a point of staying near him to try and keep him away from mischief. Bit by tiny bit she had gradually taken over her mother's role, and when she was eighteen and their mother had died she and Richard had grown closer together.

When two years later Monty had died and it had come to light that somehow or other their mother had managed to transfer all the money their father had left them to Monty, and that the inheritance that should have been theirs when they reached twenty-five had been lost by Monty in incautious dabbling on the stock market, Richard had declared since they would both have to find jobs, they would go to London where job opportunities were better. Westover Rise had had to be sold to meet creditors, as had all of the antiques they had grown up with. But once having made the decision that there was nothing to hang around for, Richard had left all the upheaval to her, and it had been she who had trudged the seemingly endless round of flat-hunting in London, she who had seen to the removal of the furniture that was of little value and hadn't been sold.

Richard had been very bitter at having to leave Westover Rise, had said he hated his stepfather's memory, but Tully couldn't help wondering if the jealousy wasn't still with him that had been there since the day Monty had moved in with them. She felt no bitterness at all towards Monty—

It went without saying that what he had done had been wrong, criminal even. He had been a rogue true, but such a charming rogue, and whatever else could be said about him, he had taken her mother everywhere with him, and had made the last years of her life exceedingly happy.

Tully went through to the sitting room, refusing to dwell on the subject. She and Richard had their health, and though the last two years hadn't exactly been a bed of roses, despite what Richard said about not waiting for Mr Burgess to retire, he had a good future ahead of him at Meachem's. He received a good salary, and should well be able to keep this apartment on once she and Howard were married—she pushed the thought away from her that Richard was always broke now—he would have to learn to take care of his money once she wasn't here to pay her half of the rent.

She picked up a sweater he had left on the settee. He would have to learn to be more tidy too, she thought, if he didn't want the place to look like a garbage dump once she had gone. En route to his bedroom, she collected his tie from off the arm of a chair while wondering if Howard would mind if she popped back here say once a week and gave the apartment a blitz. She would have to see. She didn't think Howard liked Richard any more than her brother liked him, but Howard would have to come first when they were married. Have to? Well, naturally he would, it was just that up until now Richard had been the one in need of being looked after.

It didn't surprise her on entering her brother's bedroom to see the suit he had worn to the office that day strewn anyhow across the bed. It was second nature to her to take a hanger out from the wardrobe, lift the trousers from the bed, shake out the creases and go to hang them neatly.

She muttered at her own carelessness when she went sprawling over Richard's briefcase. He'd know, she hoped, where he had left it and would have circumnavigated it, she thought, as she straightened up from her tumble. She saw she had knocked the briefcase open and went to close it, intending to place it out of harm's way.

But as her hand went down to the offending object, cold terrifying shock caused her hand to freeze in mid-air. Her eyes glued to the contents. She uttered a strangled gasp while her mind sought for some logical reason for all that money being there. There were bundles and bundles of it. Pale-faced, she sank down on to the edge of the bed. He'd brought it home for safe keeping over the weekend was her first thought, only to be chased away by the thoughts that Meachem's would have a safe, and if anything had gone wrong with the safe they would have engineers in quicker than that. The very size of Meachem's said they would have more than one safe anyway.

Still in a daze, she heard the outer door open, heard Richard's merry whistling break off as he must have noticed his bedroom door was open. She looked up, her eyes wide with hope—hope that there was a simple explanation why he should bring what must be thousands of pounds home from work, but fear at the question she had to ask had paralysed her vocal chords.

'You weren't meant to see that,' Richard said coldly from the doorway. Then heatedly, confirming for her that blackest of her suspicions, 'Oh, why the hell did you have to come in here poking and prying about, I'd have been gone by tomorrow and you wouldn't have been any the wiser.'

'Gone ...?' Her voice was less than a whisper. It hurt deeply that Richard thought she was poking and prying, but what was hurting more was the growing belief that Richard had taken money that didn't belong to him. That he had broken his employers' trust in him, for the money couldn't have come from anywhere other than Meachem's. Yet she just couldn't believe that her brother was a thief, even with him saying something about being gone. 'Where are you going?'

Richard didn't answer, he looked set to ignore any of the questions he must know were to come. 'You didn't—steal that money?' she asked, her voice barely audible. 'Richard,' she said, the numbness going from her, her voice becoming frantic, 'tell me you didn't steal it.' Her voice rose higher, 'Tell me, Richard!' she almost screamed.

'Calm down, calm down, you'll be having hysterics in a minute.'

Tully took a deep breath, knowing he was right, she *was* in danger of becoming hysterical. But this matter had to be sorted out, and now, she wasn't going to put up with any evasions from Richard—he could be in serious trouble, for God's sake. She'd get the truth out of him if it took all night, but nothing was going to be achieved by her ranting at him like a fishwife. She took another deep breath, but it did little to calm her, though her voice was not so high the next time she spoke.

'Did you take—steal—this money from Meachem's?'

Richard came further into the room, and unable to look her in the eye stared moodily at the opened briefcase. 'Why did you open it? You never have before,' he complained.

'I didn't open it, I tripped over it and it came undone— probably because it was so full,' she said tonelessly. 'Now tell me, Richard. I insist on knowing—what is all this money doing here in our apartment?'

Richard still wouldn't look at her, and she saw from the pout of his mouth that he was in a mind to be sulky. But his sulks were the least of her worries as she waited for him to answer. Then, his aggression coming to the fore, he sneered:

'Since you *insist* on knowing, Tully, I'll tell you. I pinched it, pinched the lot.' He did look at her then, and she was shaken to see he didn't look one bit ashamed of what he had done. 'With old Burgess being away I knew I'd never have another such marvellous opportunity—it was easy.'

'Easy?' Tully echoed hollowly. 'But—but your employers trusted you, Richard. You were in a position of trust. You . . .'

'Trust? Don't give me any of that trust rubbish! Our dear departed stepfather was in a position of trust too, wasn't he, but it didn't stop him from stealing what was rightfully mine.' He seemed to forget that half of it had been Tully's too, as he went on hotly, his face taking on a cynical twist, 'Well, since he took from me the only opportunity I shall ever have of doing what I want to with my life, I saw no reason why I shouldn't do something of the same—Meachem's can well afford it.'

About to protest again that Meachem's had trusted him, Tully could see before she said it that it would cut no ice with Richard, the mood he was in. 'Wh-what did you think you were going to do with the money?' she asked as calmly as she could, knowing that to give vent to her panic and start screaming at him would get them nowhere.

A light of excitement suddenly entered Richard's eyes at her question. 'I have it all planned, Tully, you've no need to worry. You'll be marrying Howard, so I've only myself to worry about.'

Tully looked at him, wondering for the first time if she had ever really known her brother. That he had stolen something that didn't belong to him appalled her, but that he could blithely imagine he could get away with it, that there would be no repercussions, that he could think the taint of everyone knowing Tully Vickery's brother was a thief wouldn't put a blight on any future happiness she hoped to have with Howard, made her think he had temporarily taken leave of his senses.

'I've got it all worked out,' he was saying. 'I was hoping you wouldn't know, of course, that way if questions are asked you wouldn't know a thing about it—you'd be perfectly innocent and wouldn't be able to tell anybody a thing.' *If* questions were asked! He must be living in a little world of his own to suppose for one moment he could steal all that money without the police being round here as soon as the theft was discovered. 'Anyway, since you're going away tomorrow, nobody will be able to question you until you come back, and by that time I shall be abroad somewhere.'

It shattered Tully that Richard could think of leaving her to face the music. She didn't know this Richard, she just didn't know him. Tears came to her eyes at the thought that he could so carelessly leave her without a word, knowing she would be worried sick about him. He seemed all set to make a clean break, though clean was hardly the best word to use, but he was prepared to go, and she had the awful idea he had no intention of sending her so much as a postcard to ease her anxieties.

'Where were you thinking of going?' she asked.

'It's better if you don't know, Tully.'

She recalled he had said something about Monty having taken away his only chance of doing what he wanted. She knew well enough what that was.

'Is there enough money there to enable you to buy enough land to set you up in the wine-making business?' she asked flatly. 'Where is it to be, Richard? France? Spain?'

Richard confirmed that she had hit the nail right on the head. 'You're too smart for your own good, Tully.'

Suddenly she had had enough. She felt there were oceans of tears she wanted to shed and she didn't know if the cause of those tears was the fact that Richard had stolen the money or because he had turned into a Richard she didn't know. She swallowed her tears, knowing that for the sake of her mother's memory if nothing else, the mother who had loved Richard and would believe no wrong of him, she was going to stop him from carrying out his plan.

'You can't do it, Richard,' she said, and was amazed to hear her voice sounding so cool, so calm, as if she was now in charge of the situation and would not be diverted from what she knew to be right.

'Can't I?' he asked, but as he saw the set look on his sister's face, his voice didn't sound as cocky as he meant it to.

'No, you can't—you can't keep that money.'

'I'm sure as hell not taking it back.'

'Then I will.' Tully said the words without knowing she had said them. But as she heard them she knew with the coldness of anger that was growing by the second within her that if Richard wouldn't return the money, then she herself would.

'Don't be daft!'

'I mean it, Richard. Either that money goes back to Meachem's or I go to the police.' At that moment she really did think she would go to the police too, and it was certain Richard believed her as his face whitened.

'You'd turn in your own brother?' he gasped in amazement.

'Yes, I would. If you make a full confession while the money is still intact your sentence will be lighter than if the police have to chase all over for you—— It might take months for Interpol to catch up with you, but make no mistake, catch up with you they would. Only it isn't going to come to that, is it?'

Richard in turn became angry, but his anger was a fury at having his plans thwarted and was no match for the icy cold anger he saw in Tully's eyes. His fury died a little, but he still tried every argument he could think of, and though Tully felt every sympathy for him when he went over his disappointment at losing his inheritance, she knew she could not allow herself to weaken. He tried sulking and whining, became bad-tempered again, but in the end he began to give way to her stronger character, though not without dragging his feet all the way.

'You can't go to the police,' he said sullenly.

'That's the last thing I want to do,' Tully told him. 'But if that money isn't returned tonight we shall have no option —they'll be on the doorstep anyway as soon as the theft is discovered.'

'But that won't be before Monday—I could be abroad by then,' Richard protested, though not with very much conviction as some of Tully's arguments began to get through to him. The idea of a week in jail, let alone the year or two he envisaged, would kill him.

'When that money has been returned to its rightful owner, you can go anywhere you like,' Tully told him flatly, wanting to forgive him already but unable to forget he had been fully prepared to disappear and leave her with all the mess at this end.

It was with very bad grace that Richard gave in to her arguments, but he was adamant that he wasn't taking it back. 'I just couldn't face it—not after all the sweat I had in getting it out, thinking every second someone would come and see me stuffing the money in my briefcase.'

If he hadn't been in such a hurry, Tully saw now, he might have got away with it, but his fear of being caught had caused him to cram the money in his briefcase so that the lock had not been as securely fastened as it might have been.

It took another ten minutes before he began fully to see that Tully's way was the only way. 'I've been a bit of a nut, haven't I? Imagining I could get away with it,' he conceded when she had been beginning to despair of ever getting through to him. 'It's well known that no one tries to put anything over on Yate Meachem without living to regret it. He'd have sent the hounds after me and wanted to do the blooding himself before he'd give up the chase.'

'So you'll take it back,' Tully said, relief flooding through her now that the past gruelling hour was over. Her relief was shortlived.

'You said you'd take it back,' he reminded her, and

seemed as stubborn as she had been in getting her own way.

Tully hadn't battled with him for the last sixty minutes only to have it all go for nothing. She could clearly see that nothing, not even the threat of a jail sentence, would get Richard within a hundred yards of Meachem's tonight.

'You'll have to draw me a map,' she said, keeping her face set, though her heart was going ten to the dozen. 'And you'll have to tell me which key is which.'

Fortunately Meachem's was less than a mile away. Neither she nor Richard owned a car, but to think of taking a taxi was out of the question. With the incriminating evidence now housed in a large plastic bag and gripped tightly under her arm, Tully pounded hurriedly along the pavements. She had never felt so frightened in her life. If a passing police car stopped her and asked what was in the black plastic bag she was carrying, she just hoped she would have enough nerve not to take to her heels and run, though she doubted they would believe she was just a kinky dresser on her way to the launderette. Everything about her shouted criminal, she felt. She had changed into black corduroy pants, had on Richard's black chunky knit sweater, had concealed her hair beneath a black beret, and not wanting to draw attention to her femininity had thought to do without her bra rather than make her breasts more noticeable than they were. It was because of the way she was attired she had decided against making part of the journey by taxi.

She was sweating profusely by the time she reached the darkened area where Meachem's had their offices. It was eerie, she was desperately afraid and would have burst into tears if she thought it would have done any good. But the time for crying was not now. She had to get inside that building, make her way to the chief cashier's office, find the safe and empty the contents of the bag into it ready for Mr Burgess to check the content's first thing on Monday morning. She had questioned why a firm the size of

Meachem's kept so much cash on the premises, and Richard had told her it was the takings from a retail outlet of one of Meachem's subsidiary companies, the paying in cash being made outside banking hours.

Tully's whole body seemed to be bathed in sweat as she neared the outer rear door and crouched low, searching for the correct key with the aid of a small flashlight she took from her pocket. Barely daring to breathe, expecting any minute to feel a hand on her shoulder, hear a voice say the equivalent of 'Hello, hello, hello,' she stealthily inserted the key in the lock. Even her hands were sweating, forcing her to place the bag down for a moment while she wiped the palms of her hands down the sides of her trousers before she could get a grip on the key to turn it. The door opened soundlessly and she wanted to cry again, only this time from fear. She had better leave the door open—not that she was likely to be discovered, she told herself bravely, for all she was sure her long brown hair would be white as snow before this night was out, but she had a feeling just the slightest unnerving sound heard in the building would have her streaking through that door like a bat out of hell.

She had studied the plan Richard had drawn, had it printed firmly in her mind before disposing of it, and now turned the corner into the corridor she was to go down. The cashier's office was right at the end of the corridor, Richard had said she couldn't miss it, it was the only door on that facing wall. Thank God it was on the ground floor, her limbs felt too weak to negotiate any stairs.

Afraid to switch on her flashlight, Tully felt her way along the walls, finding several doors but none of them the one she wanted. *What was that?* She froze, petrified, and could hear nothing. Sure her hair must be standing on end beneath the beret, she forced herself to go on. Too late now to back out, she was almost there, was fully committed.

After what seemed like a mile, but which was probably

less than fifty yards, her hand rested on the door she was seeking. It was necessary then to have some light to see which key was which, and again she bobbed down, holding her breath as the plastic bag started to slip out of her sweating hands. The bag nearly hit the floor, but she pushed her knee against it. The noise it made as she caught it with her knee and pressed it against the wooden door seemed to her terrified senses to echo endlessly in the silent corridor—she listened hard, but there was no other sound. Having selected the wrong key in her haste to complete her mission and be away, Tully stifled a groan of despair when she had to grip tightly on to the bag, hold firmly on to the flashlight and select another key from the three on the key ring.

At last she was inside, fear edging out caution as she sent the flashlight beam in the direction Richard had said the safe would be. Good, there it was. With lightning movements, her only thought to get the whole nightmare over and done with, Tully felt the cold metal of the solid-looking safe against her hands. She would love to have leant her beaded brow against it for an instant, but every second was precious. She gulped back a sob on unlocking the safe to find she needed two hands to pull back the heavy door. The door swung open—thank God for that. In feverish haste Tully opened the plastic bag and delved her hand inside. Her hand gripped some of the notes—and was careless of neatness, it was the least Richard could do to explain to Mr Burgess when they opened the safe together on Monday that he had been in too much of a hurry to stack it neatly. Mr Burgess was probably as familiar with Richard's untidy ways as she was anyway, but more important, she was much too scared to want to hang around a second longer than necessary.

The money was in her hand, she had let go of the plastic container and already had her other hand holding on to the inside of the safe when cold, icy fear, more terrible than anything she had experienced so far struck her, caused fresh sweat to break out on her forehead. Prickles of alarm rushed along the nape of her neck and down her spine. Was that a sound she heard behind her? Screaming terror had her in its grip—she wasn't in this room alone, someone else had come in . . .

Tully wasn't certain whether she actually did scream or not, but she felt the strength go out of her limbs as someone flicked a switch and electric light flooded the room. She had heard of a person's heart being heard without the aid of a stethoscope, but it was the first time she had heard her own heart knocking frantically against her ribs. The voice she heard was deep, cynical and harsh, and in no way amused as it said:

'Surprise, surprise.'

Swallowing painfully, her eyes wide with terror, Tully slowly turned round. What was in her mind she wasn't sure, probably the vague hope that she might be able to flee past her detector. But the sight that met her terrified eyes told her she was cornered. There was no way she was going to get past the rugged-looking individual standing there—he looked to be hewn out of rock. The eyes that met hers were hard and unyielding, lacking totally in compassion. She knew without having to think about it that this man was going to deal with her mercilessly, and worse, if she was going to protect Richard there wasn't a thing she could do but take what was coming to her.

A groan escaped her, seemed to come up from the very depths of her being. It had been a groan of pure despair, but if her oppressor recognised it for what it was the hardness in his eyes dimmed not one iota. Unable to hold his hard look, she flicked her eyes away as another man came into the room.

'Did they get away, Mr Meachem? The rear door is open . . .' The man, dressed in a security guards uniform stopped as he saw Tully standing there.

'There was only one, Bob, and a tiddler at that.'

'Is he armed?'

'I'm just about to find out.'

Tully didn't have time to get indignant at being called a tiddler, she was five-feet seven after all, though perhaps she did seem small to the giant of a man who was frightening her out of her mind by the firm way he was coming nearer. Then several things hit her at once. They both thought she was a man, and of all the despicable luck, the man who had caught her red-handed could be none other than Yate Meachem, the man whom Richard had said no one tried to put anything over on without living to regret it.

CHAPTER TWO

ONLY when he was barely inches from her did Yate Meachem stop. It was impossible for Tully to see the security guard with the height and breadth of him in the way. She couldn't meet his eyes and stared down at his shirt front through the open jacket of his suit. Part of her mind registered that huge though he seemed to be, and she was prepared to believe her fear of him had magnified him somewhat, there didn't seem to be any spare flesh on him. From the corner of her eye Tully saw his hands coming up and she made to dart away from him, but those same large hands came down heavily on her shoulders.

'Stay still, young fellow-me-lad, if you know what's good for you.'

She heard a movement behind him and knew the security guard was ready to take her on in the most unlikely event that she managed to wriggle out of the cement-like grip that was holding her. Her head came up and her wide brown eyes looked into a pair of blue eyes that only now when he was so close could she see had an iciness in them that boded little good for her.

'Stay perfectly still,' she was instructed again, just as though he had read in her mind that she would try and make a bolt for it anyway. 'I warn you it would take very little for me to obey the impulse to knock you senseless.'

She saw his eyes narrow as he felt her tremble. One punch from his mighty fist and her jaw would be in smithereens, she thought, and she wouldn't have moved then if the building had suddenly caught fire. Though when his hands started to go over her as he searched for any weapon she might be carrying, she thought she must have gone into rigid shock. Never had any man made so free with her body. Hot colour rushed through her cheeks as she stood immobile while those hands went firmly down behind her arms over the top of her thick sweater and all the way round her waist in case she had a gun tucked in the waistband of her trousers.

Her reaction when his hands came to the front of her was automatic and she made to push his hands away. 'Be still!' he gritted, and the next instant his hands were running down the front of her. It was less than useless to wriggle as she felt his almost imperceptible start as his hands came firmly into contact with her breasts. She was grateful his hands didn't linger any longer than it took him to confirm her sex. She couldn't look at him as her colour surged again, but knew he was giving her face close scrutiny as he stepped back from her.

'The felon's not armed, Bob,' she heard him say.

'Good,' Bob replied, 'I'll go and ring the police.'

At that Tully's eyes flew to Yate Meachem's. He stared back at her, that hard glint still in evidence. Wordlessly she shook her head, though she knew she didn't have a snowball's chance in hell of her captor letting her go.

'No, don't ring the police,' she heard him say, astonishingly. 'Go and check the rest of the building—our friend here may have a partner in crime on the premises. I'll be along to your office to see you presently.'

'You don't want me to call the police?' Bob asked behind him, and only then with his orders being questioned did Yate Meachem turn away from her.

'I'll deal with this young offender,' he said crisply.

'Yes—yes, of course,' the security guard said at once, and with another quick glance at Tully, he went and left them together, closing the door behind him.

What was he going to do with her? Tully's mind couldn't begin to think. Oh, what foul luck, another three minutes and she would have been away, no one any the wiser.

Casually it seemed to her demented eyes, Yate Meachem unhooked a chair from beneath one of the two desks in the room and sat down. The hard look in his eyes hadn't softened at all even though he must now be under no illusion that she was a man.

'I think it's about time we heard a peep or two from you, don't you?' he asked, leaning back in his chair looking as if he had all the time in the world and was prepared to sit there all night if need be.

Tully swallowed convulsively, her tongue coming out to lick her parched lips. 'What—what is it you want me to say?' she asked, her voice choked up coming from her dry throat.

'Suppose we start with your name?'

She expected him to take out a pencil and paper ready to jot down everything she had to tell, perhaps to be used in evidence against her later. But no, he appeared to have every confidence in his memory and just sat giving her that awful hard look that seemed to be taking her apart without bothering to put her back together again.

'Name?' she repeated foolishly. Then seeing his eyes narrow that she wasn't answering him quickly enough, and terrified of the consequences lest he carried out his earlier threat of knocking her senseless, 'It's Tallulah,' she said truthfully, and saw his lips firm together, clearly an indication that he didn't believe her. 'It is, honestly,' she said hurriedly.

'Tallulah what?' he rapped out.

Oh God, she couldn't say Vickery, he'd very soon know she was the sister of one of his employees.

'I ... I ...' God help her, she was so scared she just couldn't think of a name to fob him off with. Pearson came to mind, she almost said it. But no, that was Howard's name. Would it ever be hers if Howard ever found out about tonight? A smile that was more a smile of resignation crossed her features. *If* he ever found out, how could she keep it from him? It would probably be headlines in the paper tomorrow morning.

'I'm glad you find the situation so humorous,' Yate Meachem's voice broke harshly in on her thoughts as he mistook her smile. 'I don't think you fully realise the trouble you're in, Tallulah,' he said her name on a sneer. 'You may think being caught in the act of removing thirty thousand pounds from my safe highly amusing, but I think you'll be laughing on the other side of your face when I've finished with you.'

All semblance of a smile went speeding from Tully's lips as what he said sank in. It wasn't so much that he thought she was taking money from the safe, not putting it back, but the actual amount that frightened her. Richard must have been stark staring mad to think he could get away with it.

'Thirty thousand?' she said hoarsely before she could stop herself.

'You thought it was more?' Tully couldn't answer him. 'Isn't thirty thousand enough for you to risk your liberty for?'

'It—it isn't that.'

'Not much it isn't—— You're all the same,' he said, and here his voice seemed to grow harder, if that was possible. 'Grab, grab, grab, that's all you women think about. Always willing to sell yourself to the highest bidder—only you've gone one better haven't you, you little thief. You intended to cut out the middle man.'

Something had certainly soured him against women, she didn't need half an eye to see that. But what was he saying? That by stealing that amount of money she had no need to play up to any man?

'Oh, to hell with it,' he said, suddenly impatient. 'I'll

hand you over to the police. I should have done that in the first place.'

'Oh no—no, please don't!' Tully rapidly found her voice, and took a few steps towards him to beg him if need be.

'Tell me one good reason why I shouldn't? And don't invent an ailing grandmother and half a dozen starving brothers and sisters, because I warn you now I shan't believe you.'

'You're not prepared to believe anything I tell you anyway,' she fired back proudly. She had been a veritable jelly this past half hour, but if he was going to call the police anyway, she'd be damned if she'd go out kicking and screaming.

The sudden proud tilt of her head seemed suddenly to arrest him, though she didn't think her small burst of temper had done her cause the slightest amount of good.

'Believe it or not, I've been sitting here for the last ten minutes with more patience than anyone who knows me would credit, waiting for you to tell me anything that isn't a pack of lies.' He had no need to tell her he wasn't a patient man, it was written all over him. 'You've given me a false first name,' he went on, and seeing she was about to deny this, told her roughly to, 'Be quiet! God knows what your surname is, but I intend to find out—— My patience, little thief, is at an end, so start talking. Who are you? Where do you live? And how the hell did you get in here?'

She saw his eyes flick to the safe, but his expression didn't alter as he turned his glance back to her. She could see then that it would end up with the police being called, for to answer any of his questions was tantamount to putting not only herself in jail, but Richard as well.

'I can't tell you,' she said miserably, and as he stood up and made for the door, her small rush of pride deserted her, panic hitting her and she rushed to try and get to the door before him; even now there might be a chance she could escape. Fate gave a hollow laugh as she felt his arm come round her waist and she was hauled bodily away from the door as though she was some rag doll. 'Please don't call the police,' she cried as he set her to her feet. 'I'll do anything you ask, anything—but please—don't call ...' Her voice broke off as she became hypnotised by the look that came suddenly to his eyes. A look that said he had just thought of something—something had just occurred to him, and the more he thought about it, the better he liked the idea.

'Take that hat off your head,' he told her tersely.

Tully's hand went to her head. 'Take my hat off,' she repeated, wondering wildly if he had had a sudden brainstorm. She wasn't quick enough to obey him, and saw his hand whip above her, and the next thing she knew thick brown tresses of her shining hair were falling about her shoulders.

'Hmm,' he said, as if the sight of her pleased him suddenly. 'Now answer me straight and don't lie. Have you got a record?'

'Record?' she repeated, not knowing what he was getting at but having a definite feeling that if he wasn't the one who had gone mad, then it must be her.

'Have you ever been in trouble with the police?' he re-phrased impatiently.

'Of course not,' she said indignantly, then amended as his eyes narrowed, 'No—this is my first ...'

'Your first job?' He considered her for a further few seconds. 'You don't appear to be dim,' he said, then half to himself, 'Your speech is passable.' Thanks! Tully thought sarcastically, remembering the stress that had been laid on correct pronunciation at the school she had gone to and wondering if he was about to come over all Professor Higgins and ask her to repeat after him, 'The rain in Spain ...'

'I have the gravest doubts that I can believe anything you tell me,' he broke into her thoughts. 'But no doubts whatsoever that I shall be able to keep you under control should your fingers start to get sticky. Yes,' he said, his mind appearing to be made up. 'I think you'll do very nicely—very nicely indeed.'

Tully had a feeling she wasn't going to like the answer one little bit, but the question had to be asked. 'What—er —what do you have in mind?' she asked tentatively.

Yate Meachem moved from her to the safe and without answering her picked up the bag containing the money from off the floor and shut it inside the safe, then without seeming to hurry he went over to the door, the door that minutes earlier she had hoped to escape through. Then with his hand on the door handle he turned and looked steadily at her.

'You have just stated you are ready to do anything I ask provided I don't go to the police.' He paused and gave her one all-assessing look as though he had no doubts she would fall in with anything he asked of her. 'Very well,' he said, 'I'm prepared to turn a blind eye to this little caper on condition you do exactly as I say.'

Tully knew she was going to regret asking. 'Wh-what do you want me to do?' she asked, and felt the colour leaving her face as she waited for his answer.

'Oh, nothing for you to be too anxious about, I assure you,' he said smoothly, but she gained no comfort from his words. 'Nothing you haven't done many times before, I feel sure,' he said cynically. 'I need a mistress for this weekend —you'll do.' With that shattering statement, when she was almost fainting from the shock of his words, Yate Meachem opened the door and calmly left her. She still hadn't gained her breath when she heard the key being turned from the other side.

It was she who had gone mad, she was sure of it, she thought, as she fought to get on top of her rising panic. He couldn't have said what she had thought he had said, could he? There had been no emotion in his voice at all, nothing in his eyes to say he fancied her. Yet coldly, almost clinically, he had looked her over and said, 'You'll do.' You'll do to be my mistress for this weekend.

Desperately Tully looked round, her eyes going straightway to the windows. For the briefest second she thought Yate Meachem hadn't been as clever as he thought he was, thought that here was her way out. But before she got to the windows her heart dropped again in despair. Both windows had bars to them—if she had been in jail she couldn't have been more securely incarcerated.

She still couldn't believe it, that the price for her freedom, the price for not having the police called in, was for her to spend this weekend as his mis ... Oh God, what was she to do? That big rock of a man meant exactly what he had said, she couldn't doubt that. Her limbs trembling badly, Tully had to sit down. Why did he have to pick on her? she thought rebelliously. Wasn't he able to get a mistress without blackmailing someone into it, for that was what it amounted to. A picture of him as he stood by the door seemed to be etched permanently in her mind. Big, fair-haired, thirty-fiveish, though he could be older. He wasn't bad looking, not handsome certainly, but if one went for that sort of man, there was nothing repulsive about him —well, not until he looked at you with those granite-hard blue eyes anyway. It didn't add up, suddenly she was sure he never had any trouble when he went hunting, he had a virile look to him, and she had an idea any number of women would go for him, so why her? Had the feel of her when he had searched her triggered off his all-male urge?

Feeling physically sick as these thoughts chased chaotically through her mind, Tully tried to come up with the answer why. Was it just too much trouble for him to do his own hunting? Had the chase been too easy and jaded his palate? Did he want some new conquest he suspected would fight all the way?—for she was sure of one thing, she was going to fight tooth and nail to keep out of his bed.

Yet what alternative did she have? Close to tears, she strangled back that weakness. He would be looking for her to crumble, or would he? He had as good as said he didn't think she was chaste—not that she thought it would make any difference to him if she told him she was—he'd probably relish the thought of taking a virgin to bed.

It was all too much. She got up and began pacing the floor. Richard would be at home waiting anxiously for her to appear and tell him everything had gone off smoothly— oh, why had she offered to do his dirty work? She stopped her thoughts there knowing to turn against Richard wasn't going to be of any help to her. She loved her brother, there had seemed no other way out at the time, and so she had got herself into this mess. But if she hadn't interfered Richard would have been out of the country tomorrow, his ill-gotten gains going with him. She wished she could think she had been wrong to have tried to do what she had, but she knew in her heart of hearts she had tried to do the only thing possible. Fleetingly she thought of confessing everything to Yate Meachem, of imploring him not to take police action once he knew the whole of it, but the idea was shortlived. He had declared he wanted her for his mistress this weekend, and whether she brought Richard's name into it or not, she had an idea he would still demand that price for his silence—— Though why it should matter that she didn't drop her aitches, she couldn't begin to think.

Sick at heart, she looked at the windows again, as if hoping that by some miracle the iron bars placed there for security reasons had melted and her way of escape cleared. They were just the same as they had been the last time she had looked. Despairingly, Tully sank once more on to the chair, then the sound of footsteps coming along the corridor had her on her feet again. He was coming back and she had wasted too much precious time in wondering about his motives, about him, when she should have been planning her escape. All he knew of her was her first name, and he didn't believe that anyway. No, if she told him nothing else, managed to make her escape, she could be sure of one thing, he would never find her again.

Her eyes flew to the door as the key turned in the lock, then Yate Meachem was there. 'We're going,' was all he said, but it was an order for her to get moving and she knew it. Her heart set up a fluttering beat and she knew the greatest reluctance to go anywhere with him.

'Wh-where are we going?' she stalled.

Yate Meachem ignored her question. He stretched out a hand, picked up her beret from the desk and tossed it over to her. 'Cover your hair with that,' he said, 'then move.'

She didn't like the harsh way he had of speaking to her now any more than she had before, but it was the growing fear inside her, the fear of what he had in mind for her that had her doing everything she could think of, which wasn't very much, she had to own, to delay the moment.

'Why should I cover my hair?' she argued, and thought he was going to ignore her question.

'Because we shall have to walk past Bob ...' then as if she had stretched the limits of his patience too far, he took a step towards her, 'and because I damn well tell you to,' he added, and before she could take a pace backwards, he had yanked the beret out of her hands and rammed it down on her head. 'Tuck your hair in,' he instructed, and she knew he wouldn't worry about hurting her if he decided she wasn't being quick enough in obeying him. It took only seconds for her to push her hair under the hatband.

She thought he would somehow attempt to manacle her to him as he turned ready to go, but he didn't, and she hated his confidence that he knew she wouldn't get very far if she made a bolt for it. But just you wait until we get outside, Mr Meachem, she thought, as she followed him along the now illuminated corridor, just you wait!

But as soon as they reached the open rear door, her way of escape there for her, Tully could see her plan to make a break for it would come to nought. For bang in front of the door, its passenger door already being opened by the security guard Bob, stood a shining cream limousine which could belong to none other than Yate Meachem, and since he stood to the other side of her and waited until she was seated inside and Bob closed the door on her, and was at the driver's door before she could move, she knew she had lost one chance of escape. Yate Meachem knew what had been in her mind too, she didn't need the one word he cynically uttered for proof of that.

'Tough,' he said without sympathy, leaning over to fasten her into the car with what seemed to her then to be a complicated arrangement of a seat belt, a complication she knew would take her all of a precious ten seconds too long if she hoped to make a quick getaway should he stop at a set of traffic lights.

Yate Meachem offered no conversation as he called good-night to Bob and put the car in motion. She tried to get her bearings, tried to pick out land marks as they went along, but the area they were in was dimly lit, and a dreadful feeling of inertia she couldn't afford was creeping over her, and nothing seemed to be penetrating her overtaxed mind.

She had long since lost count of time and was so disorientated it could have been ten minutes or half an hour before the car was slowed down at a smart-looking block of apartments. Then Yate Meachem was driving to the covered-in parking space at the side of the building and she was noting that if the Bentleys and Rolls parked there by other owners was anything to go by, then he lived in a very exclusive area indeed.

'That's the first thing you can dispense with.'

The sound of his voice had her twisting in her seat to see what he meant. She didn't have to wait very long to find out, for she felt the beret being pulled from her head. Goodness knows what her hair looked like, for the beret had been plonked on and off her head like a yo-yo, she thought, thinking she must look like the Dulux sheepdog as she brushed her tumbled hair out of her eyes and looked around, desperately hoping for a chance to run away from him. His words came to her again. 'That's the first thing you can dispense with,' he had said—his meaning becoming only too clear. Once they were inside his apartment it wouldn't be long before the rest of her clothes were dispensed with.

'Let me go!' she begged him without knowing she had opened her mouth.

'Trying to welsh on the deal already?'

'There was no deal.'

'You said you would do anything if I didn't call the police', he reminded her. 'You still have that choice.'

'Damn you!' Tully yelled in a fury of knowing she was beaten unless she could make a break for it now.

'Such a sweet lovable creature,' Yate Meachem mocked, then before she knew what was happening, he was outside the car and locking the door on the driver's side.

Quick as a flash she moved. Her ten-second seat-belt took less than a second as, her guardian angel with her, she found the release button at the first attempt. She could have done with her guardian angel's help in finding the door catch, but at last that was found and the door open. Tully took a flying leap out of the car, only to be hauled up short as an iron grip of a hand shot out and fastened on the back of her sweater.

Stunned, not believing he had managed to move so quickly when she had thought he was still at the other side of the car, Tully stared uncomprehendingly at the man leaning negligently against the passenger's side.

'Shame,' he said insincerely.

Her first thought was to ask the ridiculous question, 'How

did you get there?' but she swallowed it. 'You swine,' she said instead.

'I'm certain you're right, Tallulah,' he taunted, 'but I've never gone back on my word to any man.'

'It's blackmail,' she spat at him, and knew he could have repeated that the choice had been hers, only he didn't.

'Try to smile sweetly at the night porter when we pass— I should hate him to think I'm bringing home some stray spitting cat.'

Tully ignored him as, her wrist firmly grasped, he locked the car from her side and strode with her panting beside him round to the front entrance. She knew he didn't care a tuppeny damn what the night porter or anyone else thought of him. Yate Meachem made up his mind what he was going to do, and to hell with anyone who didn't like it.

Well, he needn't think he's going to have his own way with me, she thought mutinously. Somehow, she didn't know how, she was going to get out of this mess, and it had to be soon. It must be getting quite late—good lord, she was supposed to be going on holiday with Howard in the morning, her case was already packed, yet it must have been hours since she had last thought of Howard.

Tully didn't even see the porter as Yate Meachem pulled her into the elevator after him. She was vaguely aware of passing a man in uniform, but her thoughts were now taken up with what Howard was going to say if she wasn't there to greet him when he arrived at the apartment at eight the next morning. She blacked her mind off as the elevator ascended higher and higher; she couldn't lose Howard, she couldn't! She thought again of appealing to the man beside her, taking a quick glance at his face as the elevator stopped and he pushed her out into the hall. One look had been enough to tell her she could appeal to him from now till Doomsday and he wouldn't budge an inch. There was no getting away from him as he took her a short way along the hall and inserted his key inside the lock of a door. She tried to hang back, but it was a wasted effort as he hauled her one-handed inside his apartment before letting go of her wrist.

'Be my guest,' he said with exaggerated courtesy as the door closed shut behind them.

She didn't answer, though she put some distance between them, wanting to have a good look round to get her bearings, but too frightened to take her eyes off him in case he should take it into his head to pounce on her.

'Drink?'

'What?'

'I asked you if you would care for anything to drink?'

So he was trying to numb her senses, was he, before he began his attack. 'I . . . I wouldn't mind a cup of coffee.'

'Suit yourself,' he said easily. 'The kitchen's through there. Don't make any for me, I'll have a Scotch.'

Glad to be away from him even if it was only in the room next door, Tully followed the direction he had given her and found herself in an extremely serviceable kitchen where no expense had been spared in getting the best. 'Don't make me one,' he had said. She hadn't been going to, not unless it was liberally laced with arsenic. Though come to think of it when she hadn't thought she would take anything he had to offer, her throat seemed to be parched dry. Fear, of course, had dried up all her saliva, but she could drink a gallon of coffee.

The coffee didn't take long to make, and she drank the first cup thirstily. Yate Meachem had made no move to come and see what she was up to, but if he was waiting for her to join him in the living room, then he was in for a very long wait. Just looking at him set her teeth on edge. She started on her second cup of coffee, wondering all the time how she could get away from him. Richard would be going frantic worrying where she had got to and although she had seen a phone in the living room, to ring him was out of the question. She had no idea how many floors up they were, but they were definitely too high up for her to think of making her exit via a window. No, she would have to watch her chance for him to leave the living room, then run like hell.

'You've been in this kitchen a long time,' said that voice she was beginning to hate. 'Cooking up some new plot, are we?' He was so near to the truth, a tell-tale colour flushed her cheeks. 'Most odd,' he commented.

'What is?' she asked, when she had already decided she wasn't going to speak to him again.

'You blushed once before this evening, I seem to remember,' he said, and she recalled straight away when that had been. He hadn't forgotten then the embarrassment she had suffered when his hands had searched impersonally over her breasts. 'You're doing it again,' he said, as with that remembrance she felt her cheeks colouring furiously. 'I should have thought you were case-hardened by now.'

'Oh, shut up!' Tully said rudely, half beside herself with worry, fear and the memory of his hands on her.

'That's more like it,' he said, ignoring her rudeness when she had been expecting him to take her up on it.

'You like your women to fight, don't you,' she said hotly. 'You ...'

'But you're not my woman, are you?' he broke in, then added silkily, 'Not yet.'

'And never will be,' she flared. 'I'd die sooner!'

'Ah, there speaks the traditional Victorian heroine,' he said mockingly. Then all trace of mockery left him, as if he had suddenly tired of the baiting game he was playing with her. 'You've spent long enough in here—I see you've finished your coffee—you can come with me.'

'Where?' she asked, her heart setting up a thunderous hammering within her.

'Why, to my bedroom—where else?'

Tully's objections which would have been fast and furious, never made themselves heard, for as though sensing she had decided her own two feet weren't going to take her within yards of his bedroom, he simply picked her up bodily in his arms, and strode out of the kitchen.

'Put me down!' she yelled, beating on his shoulders with her fists, her voice coming through after the first shocked silence, as the living room sped by as they passed through it en route.

'With pleasure,' he said, but only once they were in the room that housed a huge bed and his objective had been reached. 'By God, you could win an Academy Award for your acting,' he commented, not a bit out of breath as he dropped her unceremoniously on the bedroom carpet and stood with his back to the closed door. 'But then all you women were born with more than a touch of acting ability in you.'

'She must have hurt you like hell,' she spat at him, fury at the inglorious heap he had made of her ousting her sensitivity.

'Who?'

The word cut through the air, and as she struggled to her feet she saw a look of sheer uncontrolled hate cross his features, and a new fear swamped the fear that he had every intention of seducing her. The look on his face now, as though she had recalled to his mind the woman who had so embittered him against her sex, took on a fury that spelled nothing short of murder, and she was terrified.

'Who?' he snarled. 'Who are we talking about?'

Control seemed to come to him then from a long way off, but as though he had spent years controlling his emotions he caught at it and the livid hate she had seen in his face disappeared, to be replaced by a glacier look that said he meant to be answered.

'S-some woman soured you, didn't she?' said Tully, gaining courage on seeing he was once more in control. 'You're not interested in me as a person, or my—body as belonging to me at all,' she said, her courage growing as she thought she had found a way to get through to him. 'You see all women as the one who threw you over,' she guessed wildly, and knew she was right from the way his eyes narrowed. 'You think by using me—my b-body, you'll be able to get her out of your mind—but you never will, she still has a hold on you—you'll never exorcise her ghost that way.'

There was a dreadful silence as her voice faded away, and she dropped her eyes to stare at the carpet, knowing that if her words had not got through to him—if she hadn't been able to make him see that there wasn't a woman alive who could lay the ghost for him of the woman he must have loved and who had rejected him, then he could possibly go to the other extreme and far from making love to her, that murderous light she had seen in his eyes could have returned—even now, too scared to look at him, she knew he could be advancing towards her ready to put his hands round her throat.

Expecting at any moment to be fighting for her life, she looked up sharply at the short sound of the mirthless laugh he emitted. She saw no humour in his face as she stared at him, and there was nothing remotely to be laughed at when next he spoke.

'You're way off beam, dear little amateur psychologist.' He paused, looked her straight in the eyes with that granite-hard blue look, and said clearly, 'Now get your clothes off.'

CHAPTER THREE

TULLY had been pale before, but as his words reached her ears, she went ashen. No need to ask him to repeat what he had said, it was echoing and re-echoing in her ears.

'No!' Her refusal was point blank.

'You'd rather I did it for you?'

She backed away from him, expecting he would move after her and follow out his threat, but beyond giving her a brief impersonal look, he seemed ready to ignore her. Her brow crinkled in puzzlement; she didn't doubt he meant for her to get undressed, but when all the advantages were his, she couldn't understand why he had not made any move towards her.

'Make no mistake about it, Tallulah, I want those pants and sweater off you before I leave.'

Relief rushed in, but still she eyed him warily. 'You're going somewhere?' Unfortunately she could do nothing to stop her relief from showing, and this time there was a sort of humour in the sound when he gave a short bark of laughter.

'I must say I've had more willing women.' She didn't doubt it. 'Yes I'm going out—but,' he paused and she held her breath as she waited, 'but I want to make sure you'll be here when I get back.' If he thought being without her clothes was going to make her hang around he could think again, Tully thought, hope growing in her heart. She'd get out of here wrapped only in a bed sheet if need be. 'Now strip off,' he instructed her coolly. 'I warn you, my patience is wearing very thin.'

He turned away from her as he spoke, going to open another door to the side of him. The quick glimpse she had of aquamarine tiling told her it was a bathroom, but before she could get on her starting blocks to bolt through into the living room and out of the door towards the elevator and to freedom he was back again, tossing a white towelling robe at her and saying cynically:

'You can cover your modesty with that.'

Knowing she would have to do as he ordered, that or as he had said, have him do it for her, she stretched out her hand to take up the robe from where it had landed on the bed.

'C-can you—I mean—would you turn round, please?' It was too much to hope he would do as she asked, she could see as he cynically stared back at her that he had no intention whatsoever of complying with her request.

'Now why should I do that?' he asked as she had expected.

She wished then for the first time that she had been born a man. Oh, what wouldn't she give to knock that cynical smiling look off his face! She let out an exasperated sigh— if she had been a man she would never have found herself in this position, and anyway, even if she had been a man and had taken a swing at him, it was a foregone conclusion that anyone attempting such a feat would come off second best.

'You're wasting time,' he said when she hadn't moved, his words in themselves threatening. Tully swallowed nervously. She wasn't wearing a bra, she just couldn't pull Richard's sweater over her head and hope to get into the robe without Yate Meachem seeing something of her. He took a step nearer, his patience gone.

'Please,' she pleaded, retreating as far as she could, coming hard up against the wall. 'I haven't got anything on under this sweater and ...'

'I'm well aware of that,' he told her coldly, and as a riotous colour suffused her cheeks as she recalled how he must know, something in her frightened look, maybe it was because he had witnessed that she was again blushing, she didn't know, but he stopped suddenly and turned away from her. 'Get on with it, for God's sake,' he told her roughly, and she watched while he went to a chest of drawers, pulled one drawer open and put his hand inside.

Moving now as though jet-propelled, she hastily pulled the sweater over her head, found her fingers were all thumbs as she tried too quickly to get into the robe, but she had it round her by the time he had turned back to her. His look was uninterested as he noted that the white towelling was now covering her. But her blood seemed to freeze in her veins as she saw he had a camera in one of his hands. Oh God, he wasn't some deranged man who got his kicks out of photographing nude women, was he? For the first time in all that long evening tears welled to her eyes and rolled down her cheeks.

'Your mucky little mind just completes the picture I have of you,' he informed her harshly, his words confirming that he had read her mind accurately. 'For your information,' he said, and if his voice had been cold before it was now positively arctic. 'I want a photograph of your face—repeat face—and that, I assure you, is not because of the beauty you must know is yours and no doubt trade upon—but purely for insurance purposes.'

Tully's tears dried on her cheeks, and the strangest impulse to apologise for what she had thought smote her before she quashed it. 'Insurance?' she asked, her thinking becoming cloudy.

'I've said I'm going out. It's occurred to me that you're so desperate to get away that you'll risk going through the darkened streets of London at one o'clock in the morning dressed only in a bathrobe. Should I have cause to come looking for you I think my search will be aided if I have your face on celluloid.' Then in case she hadn't fully understood what he was saying he underlined, 'Should the deterent of my having a picture of you be insufficient to hold you here, then make no mistake about it, I shall hunt you down until I find you, no matter how long it takes.'

She had to believe him, but couldn't think about it just then. 'One o'clock?' she asked incredulously.

'It's been a long night for both of us—enough time has been wasted,' he said, and she knew then that whatever he asked of her now, she would have to obey without hesitation —he wasn't going to ask twice. 'Let me have those pants.'

He had said she was desperate, and she was, and where before she had been frightened to turn her back on him, this time she did so as with her back to him she unzipped the front of her trousers and pulled them off her legs, holding on to the dressing table for support. It was as she straightened to secure the tie belt around her before turning that she caught sight of herself in the dressing table mirror. She barely recognised the tousled-haired, wide-eyed creature that stared back at her. Her cheeks were completely without colour and her hair looked as though it hadn't seen a brush for a week as it rioted round her vulnerable-looking face. An involuntary gasp parted her lips as she saw the front of the robe had opened to reveal a goodly proportion of her swelling breasts. But it hadn't been altogether seeing herself thus that had caused her to gasp, for almost simultaneously she saw Yate Meachem's face in the mirror too, saw with that sick feeling that had never been very far away that it wasn't the reflection of her face that he was looking at.

Her movements were jerky and hurried as she pulled one edge of the robe over the other, and tied the belt in a double knot that wouldn't easily come undone. She picked up her trousers and handed them to him, saw him take up her sweater and push the two articles under his arm.

'Shoes,' he said, and there was nothing she could do but comply. 'Now sit in the middle of the bed,' he commanded, and like an automaton Tully climbed up on to the bed, clutching one hand in front of her. She wasn't going to risk the front gaping open—she was sure she hadn't mistaken that glint of interest when he had seen part of what was now respectably concealed.

'Look this way,' he ordered, and she lifted her head proudly, only to lower it again when she saw he was aiming the camera at her. 'Head up,' he thundered, and even though she knew she should be terrified of that tone, his patience a thing of the past, she just couldn't obey him.

'Very well,' he said, and there was silence for a moment. Then when her imagination was telling her he'd make her lift up her head if he had to sling it from a hook in the ceiling, she heard the sound of a click and though there hadn't been a flash, she realised he must have some new-fangled camera where no flash was necessary, though whether he had managed to get any recognisable likeness of her she had her doubts. She lifted her head, and had to screw up her eyes as they were hit by a blinding flash.

'You b ...' she began, knowing he now had the photograph of her he wanted, but the word she had been about to say was alien to her tongue and she couldn't utter it.

'Why stop there?' he asked sardonically. 'Though, contrary to your opinion, I do assure you I was conceived in wedlock.'

As he had been speaking so he was taking the snap he had of her from the camera. He waited some seconds, then peeled a strip of paper from it before surveying his handiwork.

'Perfect,' he announced. 'For a criminal you have quite a seductive mouth. I don't think I shall have to ask you to pose for me again.'

Tully gave him a speaking glance which seemed to amuse him, for the corners of his mouth twitched before he returned the camera to the drawer he had taken it from. Then with her bundle of clothes still under his arm he left the room.

By now everything that had happened was beginning to

seem unreal to her. Only hours ago she had been a perfectly normal, honest, upright citizen, working as a trans-
lator in a Government department. She had been well
adjusted, happy, looking forward to going with Howard to
spend a week in getting to know his parents, her only worry
being that Howard's parents might not like her. And now
here she was, feeling sick, tired, exhausted and dispirited.
All her hopes dashed that what she had tried to achieve
for Richard had gone so catastrophically wrong. She didn't
even have enough energy to will her limbs to get her off this
bed to see, in the event that Yate Meachem wasn't in the
living room, if she could make her escape.

And then it was too late, for he was coming back into
the bedroom, no longer carrying her bundle of clothes, the
snapshot he had taken of her no doubt in some safe place.
Just the sight of him was sufficient to have some of her
energy returning. Her flagging strength fed on her hatred of
him. As soon as he had left this apartment, and by the car
keys dangling from his fingers it wouldn't be long, though
where he was going at this hour she couldn't be bothered
to guess, but as soon as that front door closed she would
be on her feet tearing the place apart if need be searching
for her sweater, trousers and shoes.

'I shouldn't waste your time in looking for your clothes,'
he told her with that intrusion on her privacy he had of
reading her mind. 'You won't find them.'

'You have them well hidden?' she questioned, hoping
for some clue to where he had put them.

She hated that slow sardonic smile with which he re-
warded her attempted probe. 'They're not hidden at all,' he
said with false amiability. 'I've shot them down the
garbage chute—they'll be in the incinerator by now, I
shouldn't wonder.'

'You—you . . .' Words failed her.

'I am, aren't I,' he said equably. 'I should try and get
some rest if I were you,' he advised, then setting off alarm

bells within her once more, 'You have a very—exhausting weekend in front of you.'

'Go to hell!' she shot back, glad that temper was reviving her lost spirit.

'I don't intend to go there—not just yet anyway,' he said, and the way he said it, almost as if he thought she was no stranger to where he was now going, had her asking when she knew he wasn't going to tell her:

'Where are you going?' She bit her lip as soon as it was out, waiting for his sarcasm to fall. But surprisingly he did enlighten her, and what he said did nothing for the fresh rush of panic that threatened to engulf her entirely.

'You didn't try to rob my safe without the aid of an accomplice,' he said, and that hard look was back in his eyes as he said it. 'I have a very good idea who helped you in your attempt to make one of my companies thirty thousand pounds the lighter—I think it's about time I paid your fellow larcenist a visit.' With those shattering words, Yate Meachem paused only to give her a mocking smile, then he was gone.

Tully was still in a state of shock minutes after she had heard the front door close. How many precious minutes she wasted in just sitting there she didn't know, but they were minutes she couldn't afford to lose, she thought as her numbed brain began to function again. He couldn't know. He couldn't! There was nothing to link Richard with her. Wildly she looked about her as though trying to gain inspiration from the inanimate objects about her. Her eyes fell to the phone and without thinking further she moved to the side of the bed her hand outstretched to the receiver, she had to ring Richard, warn him. In the act of dialling the number she paused, then putting the receiver back on its rest realised there was no point in panicking Richard until she had thought this matter through.

If indeed Yate Meachem had got his calculations right,

and there was no saying this wasn't one almighty bluff, though it hadn't looked as though he was bluffing, then if he was on his way to see Richard it would take him some time to get there. She knew the call to Richard had to be made, that was imperative, but she needed a few minutes to think it all out first. There wasn't time to wonder why or how he had figured out that Richard had some part to play in all this mess, she must concentrate on what to tell her brother. She knew him of old, knew he would go to pieces and say more than he should if she couldn't convince him there was nothing to worry about. Having gone this far in saving his neck she wasn't prepared to let it all go to waste by Richard telling the whole of it—she knew him well, he loved the outdoors; prison would finish him.

With a calmness brought about by knowing if she couldn't come up with something little short of brilliant both her future and Richard's would be ruined, Tully forced herself to concentrate. Yate Meachem was prepared to forget all charges against her if she stayed this weekend with him. That was fact. Richard was not involved in any way at all. That was fact. But if Yate Meachem had gone to challenge him, and that was pure supposition so far, then should Richard confess that taking the money had been his crime, and his crime alone, would Yate Meachem be prepared to let Richard get away with it? Again she heard Richard telling her that no one ever put anything over on him without them living to regret it. There she had her answer. She had no doubt that once he was in possession of Richard's criminal intent, Yate Meachem would have no compunction about sending Richard to prison. Richard who got claustrophobic in their small apartment. Her hand reached for the telephone.

'Tully? Thank God—— How did it go? I've been worried out of my mind. Where the hell are you? Did you put the money back?'

Richard's panic was matching hers. Tully made a gigantic effort, swallowed and said, 'You've got nothing to worry about, Richard.'

'You put the money back in the safe?'

'Yes, I ...'

'Nobody saw you?' and before she could answer, 'Oh, hell, there's somebody hammering on the door—— Oh God, it's not the police, is it? I'll do away with myself if you've bungled it,' he ended, his voice rising.

'Calm down, calm down,' Tully said quickly. She'd heard Richard talk wildly before, but never as bad as this. She knew he didn't mean it, but he had never had the threat of a jail sentence hanging over him before. 'I told you, the money is back in the safe. I ...'

'Thank God for that!' Richard broke in over the top of her. 'Look, Tully, I shall have to answer the door—whoever it is will have the whole house awake if I don't—hang on, will you.'

'No, Richard, don't ...' she began, but it was too late. She heard the clatter as he dropped the phone down on the telephone table, and dared not hang up. She hoped and prayed his caller was not Yate Meachem. His car must have gone without his wheels touching the ground for him to have got there so quickly, though she had no idea what part of London she was now in or how far away from the apartment it was.

In an agony of suspense she waited for Richard to come back and tell her who his caller was—who else would call at their apartment at this time of night? She willed Richard to keep a cool head. She couldn't hear a sound, but knew as the apartment door led directly into the sitting room that Yate Meachem must be standing not too far away from the phone.

'You still there, Tully?' She could hear the disquiet in Richard's voice; it confirmed for her who his visitor was before he said, 'Mr Meachem has just called—apparently my keys to the office have been found and he wants to know when I had them last.'

Oh God, those keys!—she had left them dangling in the safe, she'd forgotten all about them. She saw it all now. Yate Meachem had gone over and closed the safe, removed the keys and with those same set of keys he had locked her in the cashier's office, presumably while he had gone into the security guard's office to check on the list of names and addresses of authorised key-holders.

'Tully?'

'It's all right, Richard, now calm down,' she said, her mind working overtime. 'Er—tell Mr Meachem you must have dropped your keys on your way out of the building——' she thought rapidly, then added, 'Mr Meachem has probably had the contents of the safe checked and it must be all there or he would have contacted the police, wouldn't he?'

'Yes—yes, of course—you're right.' His voice began to sound less agitated.

'You'll have to apologise and say you'll be more careful in future,' said Tully, talking for the sake of talking—anything to get him to appear more normal, Yate Meachem wasn't going to miss that Richard had sounded apprehensive.

'Yes—yes, all right.' Thank God he sounded calmer. 'Where are you, Tully?'

She could have done without him asking that, particularly since if she told him, he would disintegrate. Where the dickens could she say she was that wouldn't have him all excited again?

'It was still early when I'd—finished that little job,' she said, inspiration coming out of thin air, 'so I came over to Howard's. He thought as we've got such a long way to go tomorrow we'd save half an hour on the journey if we went straight from his place.'

Tully had to go and rinse the sweat from her moist palms

when she had replaced the receiver. For all she had never stayed the night at Howard's before, Richard had taken everything she had told him as gospel. There was no reason why he shouldn't believe her, of course, she couldn't remember ever having lied to him before. If only he could keep his head while he was talking to Yate Meachem, that was all she asked.

She left the bathroom and walked into the living room, noticing for the first time that it was roomy and comfortable-looking, but definitely all male with its brown leather upholstered furniture, brown carpet and stark white walls. Her mind racing, she sat down in one of the easy chairs.

Clearly there could be no thought of escape now. Even if that was possible, and she still thought she had enough nerve to try and get home dressed as she was—the robe came down to below her knees—Yate Meachem's sixth sense had taken him straight to Richard. She could still go away with Howard for a week she supposed ... Oh God, Howard—how was she going to ... She put Howard firmly out of her head. Thoughts of Howard would only cloud the issue, though she would have to get in touch with him somehow and let him know she wouldn't be going with him after all. She choked back a sob that rose to her throat and forced herself to concentrate on the more immediate problem.

If she did manage to get away, she would live in dread of Yate Meachem turning up on her doorstep. The thought rushed in that perhaps she and Richard could move, perhaps Richard would leave his job, Yate Meachem would never find them—but the thought had to be cancelled out. If she wasn't here when he got back there were no two ways about it, he would go straight back to Richard. He must have heard Richard calling her Tully, one would have to be thicker than two short planks not to make the connection between Tallulah and Tully, and heaven alone knew what Richard had let slip anyway. No, she couldn't go back to the apartment, that would be the first place he would look for her, and she felt certain that even if she did get away, left London for a week to go to Scotland with Howard, Yate Meachem would be there waiting for her when she got back. Richard would crack, she knew he would, if Yate Meachem, his patience burnt out, was allowed to get at him while she was away.

Tully was sitting staring into space when Yate Meachem returned. She had jumped when she had heard his key in the lock, but had herself under control when the door closed behind him. She didn't move when he came further into the room. She saw the dark material of his trousered legs and knew he was standing in front of her but was in no mind to speak to him.

'Sulking, Tully?' Her heart sank and she didn't answer him. So he *had* made the connection between Tallulah and Tully, it had been too much to hope that he wouldn't. 'You're a very wise girl,' he said, and because she had no idea what he meant by that, this time she did raise her head to find him looking mockingly down at her.

'Wise?'

'It had crossed my mind that you might take it into your head to make a hasty exit. Since I've already told you that in that event I would hunt you until I found you, it would have been very unwise for you to have done that—wouldn't it?' He paused, then added, 'Miss Vickery.'

Tully looked down again, but not before he had seen her eyes widen in alarm that he now had her surname neatly on file.

'It was thoughtful of you to ring your brother and tip him off—I'm sure he appreciated it.'

She hated that cold sardonic voice, and her hands clenched in her lap. What wouldn't she give to beat her fists against his mocking head! But these instincts had to be controlled.

'Richard had nothing to do with—with what I did to-night,' she stated firmly.

'No?'

'No.'

'You're telling me you just lifted the keys from his dressing table or wherever, took it into your head that you could do with some extra cash for your holiday ...' Oh lord, Richard had told him about that, had he—she wished she knew what else he had told him, '... and without assistance from your brother, you just waited until it was dark and went along to do your dirty deed?'

'Yes.' Her voice was less firm now as she heard that harsh note entering his voice. Then defiance she hadn't thought she would ever feel, if even in her wildest imagination she had ever thought to find herself in this situation, which she hadn't, stormed through her, and she raised her head, refusing to flinch at the flint-like look in the blue granite that looked back at her. 'And I nearly got away with it, didn't I?' she challenged. 'Another three minutes and I would have done.'

'No way,' he contradicted her coldly. 'Even without the security devices I employ, your bungling amateur attempt could be heard all over the building.'

She hadn't thought she had made that much noise, she was sure she hadn't. The only noise she could recall from that whole nightmare had been when she had knocked the bag against the door and held it in position with her knee. But that thought was incidental as a more terrifying thought rushed in.

'Security devices?' Her voice came out in a strangled whisper she was contemptuous of, but could do nothing to alter. 'What security devices?'

'Surely you don't expect me to tell you, a would-be thief, that?'

'You ...' her voice died, and she tried again. 'You

haven't got concealed cameras?' she asked, the sudden idea that the whole performance from the moment she had turned that key in the lock at Meachem's was on film making her almost go under. She waited agonisingly for him to answer, and just when she thought he was going to ignore her question, he laughed scoffingly.

'Not so defiant now, Miss Vickery, are you?' he jibed. 'You must be in a panic if you've forgotten that I've taken a photograph of you since we left the building where you think I might have my own private film show. Not quite as clever as you think you are, are you?'

His jibing tone was lost on her as relief flooded in. But the defiance he had seen and had thought gone from her came once more to her aid, waving like a banner of pride that she wasn't going to allow him to completely demoralise her.

'All you've got to say that I was there is your word against mine?' She knew it was useless to try, but at least she wasn't going under without a fight.

'You're forgetting surely about Bob, the security guard?'

'He'll never recognise me—anyway he thinks it was a man he found in the cashier's office.'

All at once she was getting very excited, and couldn't think why she hadn't thought to take this line of attack before. There was no proof that she had been there, none whatsoever; even the clothes she had worn had gone. They weren't to know Richard hadn't originally put the money in that plastic bag in the first place, and since none of it had been taken, Yate Meachem just didn't have a thing against her.

Seeing he had moved away from her and was just standing there, an inscrutable look on his face, she thought she could safely stand up without coming into too close contact with him. It was a pity she wasn't dressed to kill. She rather thought having bare feet and wearing his bathrobe detracted something from her exit line, but feeling better now than she had for goodness knew how many hours, Tully got to her feet.

'So,' she said with a shade more confidence than she was actually feeling, 'if it's all the same to you, I think I'll go home.' She wished she hadn't looked at him then. She was sure there was nothing funny in what she said, though maybe she would see the funny side of it much later, but he looked for all the world as though it was all he could do not to burst out laughing.

She made it as far as the door, could feel her heart pounding all the way. It was all so easy—she had called his bluff and won. Her hand was actually on the door handle when he said the three syllables that had her frozen.

'What? Wh-what did you say?'

She turned, her eyes going huge as that dreadful sick feeling washed over her again. Her exhilaration had been shortlived.

'I said fingerprints,' he repeated, and that mocking smile was back. 'You've told me it was your first break-in, and I'm inclined to believe you, little amateur. You really should have worn gloves, Miss Vickery, and while I'll allow there might have been the odd occasion when you may have visited your brother in the building, visitors are just not allowed in the cashier's office, and for the life of me I can't see any way your fingerprints could have got on to the *inside* of the safe—as I recall you had your hand pressed up against the inside of the safe when I turned on the lights.'

He didn't have to ask her to leave the door and come back into the room. Tully's feet moved without her knowing it, and she returned to the chair she had vacated so loftily only minutes ago, silently calling him all the names she could lay her tongue to.

'You really must stop seeing me as the villain of the

piece,' he told her smoothly, as though he was reading her mind. 'Didn't anyone ever tell you that crime doesn't pay —or to paraphrase that—that crime has to be paid for?'

Her senses sent up a violent reaction. So he was back to that again! Oh, surely he didn't mean it—that she should be his mistress for this weekend? Her senses became even more alarmed when he stood up and said easily,

'Well, I don't know about you, Tully Vickery, but I'm ready for my bed.'

Her eyes flew to his and it did little for her feelings of disquiet that the hard look had gone from his eyes. Dear heaven, was he about to try to seduce her ...?

'I ... I'm not tired,' she said, when she was very near to dropping from the exhaustion this night had woven on her.

'Perhaps tomorrow I shall feel more like working a cure on your insomnia,' he said, and to her relief and amazement he moved towards the bedroom. 'But for tonight I think I'll sleep the few remaining hours till dawn.'

Tully hardly dared to believe that for tonight at least he wouldn't attempt to molest her. His bedroom door was firmly closed, all was silent. She waited what seemed an age, but was probably no more than half an hour, and only then, when no sounds could be heard coming from the bedroom, did she begin to unwind. But she dared not relax completely, dared not make herself too comfortable and risk falling asleep. As soon as the time came round to what might be called a reasonable hour, she would have to ring Howard.

In an endeavour to keep awake she went into the kitchen and as quietly as she could made herself a cup of coffee. The hours until dawn arrived were, she thought, the longest she had spent, and she still had no clear idea of what she was going to tell Howard. Countless ideas came to her, but each one had to be discarded as not holding water. It was going to be a beautiful day, she thought absently, as the sun started to creep over the horizon. She wished she knew what the time was, but there wasn't a clock to be seen anywhere.

When she thought it must be getting on for seven she picked up the telephone, hoping with all her heart that the slight pinging sound it made wouldn't transfer to the phone in the bedroom and waken Yate Meachem. If she never saw him again it would be too soon. She dialed for time information. No point in getting Howard out of bed if it was not as late as she thought it was. She had no idea whether he was the grumpy sort first thing in the morning, she would need all her tact as it was, so it would be better if he was already up when she called. It was 'Six-thirty precisely,' she was informed. Replacing the phone, she swallowed hard. She didn't want to lie to Howard, but he would never understand if she told him the truth. Yet she had to tell him something—if he called round for her as arranged, then apart from any other consideration, Richard would know she hadn't been where she had said she was last night.

Tully took a deep breath, picked up the phone again, and dialled Howard's number. Somehow she had to get through this weekend, get through it and come out unscathed. She had enough problems without Howard adding to them. She now had her story prepared, pray God he believed her.

CHAPTER FOUR

THE ringing tone went on for some time, which did nothing for Tully's agitated feelings as she decided Howard must still be in bed. The ringing stopped, and her heart plummeted as she heard Howard, slightly tetchy, give his number, but for a moment her fears that he *was* a grouch first thing in the morning took a back seat as her ears picked up a definite click. For one stunned second her nervous thoughts led her to believe that Yate Meachem had picked up the phone in the bedroom and that he was listening in, and her voice died on her. Then Howard's voice, with a petulance she had never heard in his voice before, was asking, 'Who's there?' and fearful that he might hang up on her, she forgot all about the man in the bedroom.

'Howard—it's me, Tully.'

'What are you ringing for? I shall be picking you up at eight.' The petulance was still there, and she wished she could say something other than what she had to say, but she couldn't.

'I'm sorry, Howard—— I ... I can't make it.'

'Can't make it! What are you talking about? What can't you make?'

'I can't come on holiday with you,' Tully said, then before he could say anything further, she went on, 'You know when I told you a little about my job—well, I explained then that there's a rule that states that if necessary leave can be cancelled——' she swallowed, that part was true at least. 'Well, I heard late last night that there's a bit of a flap on and ... and my holiday has been cancelled.'

'Cancelled?' Howard sounded incredulous that a Government department could dare to spoil his holiday plans.

57

'It can't be cancelled—my parents are expecting us—it's all arranged!'

'I'm sorry, Howard,' Tully apologised again, hating herself more than Howard could be hating her at this moment. 'You know I was looking forward to meeting your parents, but there's not a thing I can do about it.'

'Well, I call it a damn poor show. Why didn't you ring me last night? It would have been the decent thing to do.' He really sounded quite pompous, but she couldn't blame him.

'I would have done,' she improvised, 'but it was late when I heard and you said you were going to have an early night.'

Howard couldn't argue against that. 'Well, I call it a damn poor show,' he said again. 'It's not even as if your job is all that important. Surely your being there isn't going to make any difference?'

It hurt that Howard didn't think her job was all that important. It wasn't, of course, but she was good at it and had soon been promoted to a higher grade, but she hadn't thought he had looked on her job that way.

'I'm sorry,' she said for the umpteenth time.

'But . . .' Howard seemed ready to protest again, and suddenly, for all he was so dear to her, she had had enough.

'I can't do anything about it, Howard,' she said, just a shade more sharply than she meant to, but she was bone tired and was hardly thinking straight. 'And I can't tell you anything about it . . .'

'I can't think of anything you might know that could be classed as a State secret,' Howard cut across her. 'Even if your job does have security clearance.'

She could see they were on the brink of an argument, but she couldn't afford to let him rile her. 'I'm sorry,' she said, thinking she should get a record made of those two words. 'Would you apologise to your parents for me—— Shall I write . . .?'

'Don't bother,' Howard snapped.

At any other time Tully would have placated him gently, but his attitude about her job, even if he was right and she didn't handle any State secrets, plus her tiredness and the culmination of the last ten or twelve hours had got her on the raw.

'I'll see you when you get back,' she said quietly at last.

'Possibly,' Howard said in such a way that for the first time she began to doubt that he loved her as much as he had said he did. Her pride took over at that point.

'I see.' She paused while part of her mind was saying this couldn't really be happening—they'd been on the brink of getting engaged, hadn't they? 'Goodbye, then, Howard.' She didn't wish him a happy holiday—she didn't think he would appreciate it.

Putting down the phone, she wandered over to the settee. Her story to Howard had been believed, but he hadn't accepted it as well as she had hoped he might. Lord, she was tired! She sank down on the settee, her mind in a whirl. She had no intention of going to sleep, was of the opinion that her thoughts were too chaotic for her to ever find rest, but inside a very few minutes her eyelids were coming down. She lifted her feet on to the settee to be more comfortable, and five minutes later she was dead to the world.

Yate Meachem came silently from his bedroom. He saw at once that his guest was asleep on the settee, and stood for some moments studying her. Her hair was a tumbled mass of thick brown waves, the lashes that had fanned down were thick, luxurious and too long to be real, but he could see they were—could see too that she was exhausted. Her face was solemn in sleep that did not detract from the beauty that was hers, the hollow cheeks, the dainty nose, the seductive mouth with its full lower lip. As silently as he had come, he left her.

Tully's nose twitched, she opened her eyes, was briefly happy, then remembered where she was. Richard, Howard,

Yate Meachem all tumbled into her waking brain, and she sat up wondering that she had been covered with a blanket while she slept. She checked to see that she was still wearing the robe she had put on—how long ago? The smell of bacon cooking made her aware that she wasn't in the apartment alone. In the kitchen Yate Meachem was cooking his breakfast.

On the point of wishing she had some clothes, wishing she dared take a bath without being disturbed, a sound made her raise her head and she looked to see a freshly shaved Yate Meachem standing there looking supremely confident, large and all male. Remembrance of what he had in mind for her stormed in and hot colour rushed through her cheeks. But if he noticed her heightened colour, he chose to ignore it.

'Hungry?' he enquired urbanely.

Tully shook her head. 'No,' she said shortly, and as he stood watching her, seeming to expect her to say something more, she found herself saying, when she had no intention of getting into conversation with him, 'I couldn't eat a thing.'

He left his position by the door and came to stand about a yard or so away from her, his eyes studying her face with its smudged shadows beneath her eyes.

'Perhaps you'll feel more like eating once you're bathed and dressed,' he suggested, and she was struck by the harsh sort of kindness in his voice. It was as though he was feeling some regret he didn't want to feel, she thought, then dismissed the idea that he would feel he had anything to regret and that she must have imagined there had been a softening in him.

'Perhaps I would,' she told him coldly, not prepared to warm to him at all if he still intended to carry out his threat. 'But first of all I would need some clothes to put on —my other things went down the garbage chute, I believe?'

'Your clothes are in the bedroom.'

'You didn't dispose of them?' She could hardly believe it, and hated him afresh for all the time she had wasted waiting for dawn to come when she could have been searching for them.

'Your pants, shoes and sweater went down the chute as I told you,' he informed her smoothly. 'But your *holiday* suitcase plus your handbag is in the bedroom.'

'Holiday suitcase?' She was astounded. How had he managed ...

'You left your suitcase in the living room of your apartment,' he reminded her, when she didn't need any reminding. She had packed everything well in advance, part of her eagerness to start her holiday with Howard, she supposed. Only last night she had put her suitcase with her handbag on top behind the settee all ready to pick up this morning, her bedroom being no larger than a closet and there being the constant threat of her going head over heels while it stood in there.

'Your brother tripped over it as I was leaving. He explained that you were spending the night with your boyfriend,' was there a slight emphasis there? As though he thought it was a regular occurrence for her to spend the night with Howard? There wasn't time for her to think further, for he was saying, 'Your brother said you intended to make an early start, but as you would have to call back for your case he would either have to take a taxi and bring your case and bag to you or you would have to return for them. I asked him where said boy-friend lived and when he told me I said as I would be passing that way about seven this morning, I'd drop them in for you.'

What a mind he'd got! And she had hoped to outwit him. He had successfully stopped Richard from wondering what on earth was going on. And at the same time, since it looked as though he didn't intend her to spend the whole weekend dressed in his robe, he had ensured that she had something to wear that didn't entail his going out and buying something for her. She didn't feel she could thank him, even though she thought she might begin to feel more normal dressed in her own clothes.

'Unless you intend to sit around like that for the rest of the day might I suggest you go and get bathed and changed?'

Tully was on her feet. The idea had infinite appeal and since it was his suggestion that she dressed, she found some small comfort that at least he couldn't have any intention of carrying out his vile threat until this evening. But she wasn't sure how far she could trust him and made no move to go to the bathroom.

'Something the matter?'

As if he cared. 'Y-you won't come in—I m-mean when—I'm in the bath?' She knew her face was showing her uncertainty but could do nothing about it. This towering man had the power to frighten the life out of her.

He looked at her steadily for a long moment. 'No,' he said harshly at last, 'I won't come in.' And then, his voice softening to add sardonically, 'Not unless you would like me to come and wash your back?'

Unspeaking, she left him. She saw her suitcase as soon as she opened the bedroom door. It seemed a year away since last Thursday evening when she had packed it with such happy anticipation. She recalled the telephoned conversation she'd had with Howard—how long ago? She had no idea how long she'd slept—she hoped with all her heart that Howard had forgiven her when he came back from Scotland, had no doubts that he would go without her; his parents were looking forward to seeing him.

Unsnapping the locks on her case, she took out fresh underwear, her new jeans bought specially for her holiday and a white sweater. There was a push bolt on the inside of the bathroom door, and she rammed it home feeling some small security in the action, even though she knew that if

Yate Meachem felt so inclined to go back on his word, he wouldn't have much trouble if he cared to put his shoulder against it.

She spent some time over her toilet, enjoying the heated water lapping over her body in a bath that was almost large enough for her to swim in. It would have to be large to fit him, she thought, then tried to keep her mind off him because somehow she had to concentrate all her efforts on thinking and planning on how she was going to keep from sharing that oversized bed with him tonight.

Knowing she had spent far too long in her bath, and the sudden panicky feeling hitting her that if he thought so too she might yet hear a shoulder come crashing against the door, Tully stepped out and hurriedly began to dry herself. It was amazing, she thought as she pulled on her jeans, what clothes could do for one's equilibrium. She felt much better, even felt hungry. Not wanting to look in any way attractive she decided against wearing make-up, completely unaware that her face had a beauty that was there regardless of cosmetics.

Leaving the bathroom, she saw she had the bedroom to herself and set about brushing the tangles out of her hair, then finding a couple of rubber bands in her case she made two bunches of her hair. There, she thought with satisfaction, there was nothing at all sexy in her appearance. She was as slender as a boy and though her breasts were of average size, her loose sweater did nothing, she thought, to draw attention to them. Feeling perhaps she would be unwise to delay any longer, she opened the bedroom door.

Yate Meachem had obviously breakfasted, and was ensconced in one of the easy chairs reading the morning paper. As Tully came further into the room he put the paper down and stood up, his eyes going slowly over her. Had she known it, she looked young, vulnerable, and totally innocent standing there, and she could see no reason why his lips should firm in an angry line, not unless he was re-calling of course that he thought she had tried to rob him of thirty thousand pounds.

'How old are you?' he asked grittily.

'Twenty-two,' she answered, startled into replying by the unexpectedness of his question.

'You don't look it. What made you do your hair in that ridiculous fashion?'

About to say, 'Don't you like it—I dressed it this way specially for you', she realised that would sound much too provocative. 'I always wear it this way on Saturdays,' she lied, and saw the harsh look leave him, and thought with wonder that her answer had amused him as she watched the corners of his mouth start to lift before they were severely repressed.

'Feeling hungry now?'

She was starving, but wouldn't give him the satisfaction of knowing it. 'I could eat a slice of toast.' She took a step towards the kitchen. 'May I help myself?' she asked politely.

'Feel free.'

Tully wasted no further time in getting away from him. She wanted to, needed to, keep a hostility going between them. It went without saying that he just hadn't got a better nature she could appeal to, and if he was set on having her for his mistress then it was going to be a fight all the way.

She felt better for having a slice of toast inside her, but her instinct to ask him if he wanted a cup of coffee when she poured her own was strangled at birth. She wasn't go-ing to yield an inch. Her stomach turned over when look-ing up after taking a satisfying gulp of her coffee she saw he had come silently to the kitchen and was blocking the doorway.

'Why haven't you got a clock?' she asked aggressively, the need to say something paramount.

'Because I don't like them,' he answered, and she was

glad to see he didn't intend to come any nearer. 'A watch is sufficient for my needs.'

She guessed then that he put in many working hours and that clock-watching wasn't his forte. If he hadn't been working last night ... 'Well, would you mind consulting your watch now and telling me what the time is?'

She saw his eyes narrow at her tone, caution telling her she had better watch her step. She swallowed a knot of apprehension when he left his position by the door jamb and came nearer to her. Involuntarily she flinched back when he lifted his arm and she could have wished he hadn't guessed that she had been afraid he had been going to hit her.

'It's eleven o'clock,' he told her, and while it was sinking in that it was much later than she had thought, he was saying, 'Keep up your cheeky attitude, Tully, and I may yet deliver the hiding you appear to be expecting.'

'I don't doubt it,' she answered him back, when she knew it would be better for her if she kept quiet. 'You're dying to take a swipe at me, aren't you?'

'Hitting you wasn't quite what I had in mind,' he said meaningfully, and suddenly there was tension in the air as his hands came down one on each of her arms and he lifted her bodily from the pine chair she was sitting on and stood her to her feet. 'I have an idea there's a better way to tame you than by pugillistic methods.'

He still had hold of her two arms and she tried desperately to struggle free as she felt herself being pulled inexorably nearer. His face was so close she could see that his eyelashes were darker than the fair hair on his head and she went rigid in his grip, her eyes widening in fear that he didn't intend to wait until tonight before he began his assault on her. He must have read the fear in her face, and his mouth could have been only inches away from hers when a look of distaste, whether for himself or her she couldn't know, came over his expression, and he pushed her roughly away, turning his back on her.

'Behave yourself, Tully, or your hour of reckoning will come sooner than you anticipate,' he grated, and left her to sink back on to the chair, her limbs trembling so badly they wouldn't hold her.

She had just learned one very salutary lesson. Yate Meachem was not prepared to put up with any cheek from her. And something else she had learned, or so she thought —he had enough assurance about him to take her any time he wanted, but it seemed he had his time planned, and that time had not yet arrived. She was still sitting there when he came back some little time later.

'Since you're so concerned with the time, you'd better have this,' he said, and pushed a man's wrist watch over to her.

Tully looked at him then, saw from his face that he wasn't feeling any friendlier to her than he had before, and couldn't understand why then he was lending her the watch. Probably because he envisaged growing fed up with her asking the time every five minutes, she thought, but the question rose to her lips:

'Won't you need it yourself?'

'It's a spare.'

She saw the watch on his wrist, gold, thin and out of her price range. 'Thank you,' she said gently, putting the watch he had pushed across the table to her ear and checking that it was going. She looked up to see he had followed her every move, read in his eyes that he would have little to do with anything that didn't fulfil the purpose it was designed for, and strapped the watch to her delicate wrist, before pulling down her sleeve on the timepiece that was much too large for her.

A brooding silence hung between them, but she certainly wasn't going to be the one to break it. She was going to be very careful what she said in future. The silence seemed to go on for an age. What he was thinking about she couldn't begin to guess. She wanted to check the time again by the watch he had given her, but stifled the impulse, not wanting to draw his attention to her. Then suddenly she felt those piercing blue eyes directed on her and felt herself growing hot. Oh lord, what was coming now? He had something to say to her, she was sure, but whatever it was she was certain she didn't want to hear it.

'Do you have anything resembling a party dress in your case?'

Party dress? That was the last thing she had expected to hear! Nightdress, yes, but party dress? 'Why?' she asked, when all reason told her it would be better if she gave him a straight yes or no.

He gave a long-drawn-out sigh as though he was thoroughly fed up with her, and that gave her enormous satisfaction. 'Because,' he said carefully, as though trying to hang on to his temper, 'if you haven't got one, I shall have to go out and get you one.'

Tully was intrigued. Even supposing she would allow him to purchase clothes for her, and if she had any say in the matter she was certain she wouldn't, why on earth should she need a party dress? About to ask, she took one look at his face and decided against it.

'I do have one, as a matter of fact,' she told him, then curiosity getting the better of her caution, 'Why—why do I need one?'

'I had thought you were quite bright,' he said sarcastically. 'Do you not usually wear a party dress when you go to a party?'

'I'm going to a party?'

'To be more precise, *we* are going to a party.'

'You're taking me to meet some of your friends?' She couldn't believe it. It didn't add up. She had probably moved in a circle similar to his before she had come to London, so it wasn't that that bothered her, but he thought she was nothing short of a common thief, surely he wasn't going to take her where he would have to risk her stealing from his friends? Her look said it all without her having to press the point.

'I'm taking you to meet my family,' he floored her by saying, then carried on, 'I don't want to have to physically check either your belongings or you personally when we get back here, so if you have any ideas of doing a spot of pilfering while we're there I advise you to think again. You won't get a second chance with me.'

By that he meant he wouldn't hesitate to call the police if he found any of his family's possessions in her luggage, but she wasn't bothered about his insults or his insulting tone just then. All she saw was that they were going among other people. She wasn't going to be alone with just him and his ideas of what he was going to do to her once night fell—she might even have a chance to enlist the aid of someone. She wasn't sure how this could be achieved, for to escape from him was out of the question, she had no way of knowing that he hadn't already had her fingerprints lifted and photographed, or photographed and lifted.

'I see the idea of getting away from this apartment appeals to you—or is it just me you're hoping to get away from?'

He saw too much altogether in her opinion. 'Every girl likes the idea of a party,' she said evasively. 'And anyway, I can't get away from you, can I? Not while those fingerprints remain on your safe.'

'You *are* as bright as I thought,' he said, and returned to the subject they had been discussing. 'We'll have a spot of lunch here first, I think, and be on our way about three.'

'Three? Er—have we far to go, then?'

'My family home is about an hour's run—you'll have plenty of time to change when we get there.'

'Oh.' She regretted she couldn't think of anything smarter to say in reply to that, but he had the uncanniest knack of taking her feet from under her. 'I'll need a small bag or something to put my dress, make-up, that sort of thing in,' she said, warming to the idea of getting away from here if only for a short while.

'You can take your case—we'll be staying the weekend.'

'Weekend?' she repeated, wishing she hadn't when he favoured her with one of his cynical looks.

'We may stay longer, who knows,' he informed her, and she knew then that they wouldn't, he was just delighting in frightening her. 'You have nothing special to come back for, have you? Your brother thinks you'll be away for a week.'

'My brother also thinks I'm away with Howard,' she snapped, the game he was playing with her needling her. 'I'm supposed to be on holiday with him,' she added heatedly.

'My dear Tully Vickery, if I report your night-time activities to the police, and I may,' he threatened, and that she could have done without, 'your holiday will stretch for longer than a week, I can promise you. And I doubt they would allow you to have dear Howard in your bed to comfort you where they would put you.'

The excitement that had rocketed through her that she would soon be leaving this apartment fell flat as his words reached her. She felt again that same churned-up feeling she had experienced last night and early this morning.

'Don't you think you've punished me enough already?' she said dully. 'Thanks to you and your insistence that I stay with you this weekend, the likelihood of my ever marrying the man I love is receding further and further away.'

'You're engaged to be married?' The question surprised her by its sharpness. Surprised her into answering honestly.

'N-not exactly,' she confessed huskily. 'But until I told Howard I wasn't going with him he was in love with me. Oh!' she said, suddenly remembering that Yate Meachem didn't know anything about that phone call.

'I know you rang him first thing this morning.'

'How . . .?' she began, then remembered the click she had heard. But before she could challenge him about it, he was saying uncaringly:

'I listened in—to both calls,' he told her. 'I must say the second call was much more interesting than the first. I fully expected you to try and contact the boy-friend—you'd have to let him know something, otherwise he would have called at your apartment this morning, and that wouldn't have suited you one bit, would it?' He knew it all, didn't he, Tully thought mutinously, holding hard on the desire to hit that clever face that could reason before she could blink. 'And if his love for you is such a poor thing that just the fact of your having to back out of your holiday arrangements can kill it, I shouldn't have thought it was worth having. I thought your excuse for not going was masterly, by the way, though how the hell you ever got a security clearance beats me.'

'Until now my character has been without a stain,' she said, and knew it was stalemate when he gave her a disbelieving look and went from the kitchen.

Lunch was eaten in comparative silence. As a meal it satisfied her pangs of hunger but didn't require any culinary brilliance—tinned potatoes, grilled steak, tomatoes and frozen peas. Barely a word was spoken between them, and she was glad about that. Yate Meachem seemed preoccupied with his own thoughts, and whatever they were didn't appear to be very pleasing. Tully wondered if his thoughts had anything to do with her, and hoped not, even though she hadn't thought she would be anything other than delighted that his thoughts were obviously not happy ones.

He surprised her when she began to tackle the washing up, by picking up a tea-towel. 'I can do that,' she said without thinking, then clamped her lips hard together. Already she had forgotten she wasn't going to speak to him unless spoken to. He carried on drying up as though she hadn't

spoken. She wondered then, since he had unbent suffici-
ently to take over his share of this household chore, if there
was any chance of her appealing to him to let her go. She
would have to be very tactful about it, she saw. To ask him
bluntly would have him giving her an equally blunt no.
Yet since he disliked her so heartily she reasoned he would
have scant satisfaction if he tried to do with her what he
had so clearly stated.

'Your family ...' she began, cursed the need to clear her
throat and began again. 'Your family won't be expecting
me, will they?'

If Yate Meachem already saw where her indirect ap-
proach was leading, he gave nothing of it away, but carried
on with drying the plate in his hand.

'What makes you think that?'

'Well, I mean—how can they? You didn't—hadn't met
me until last night,' Tully warmed to her theme. 'Won't
they think it a little odd, bringing a girl into the house
they've never heard of before?'

'I shouldn't think so for a minute,' he said, almost de-
flating her completely, though she wasn't prepared to give
up yet.

'But,' she nibbled her lip seeking inspiration, 'but surely
they won't want me there—I mean ...'

'Leave it, Tully,' his voice broke in, harsh over the top
of hers. 'You can wriggle all you like, but make no mistake
about it, I've decided you're coming with me, and that's
exactly what you'll do.'

She knew she was defeated, felt despair growing in her
that there was no way out, but still she wasn't going to let
him see how defeated she felt.

'Very well, Mr Meachem,' she said defiantly, throwing
the dishcloth down on the draining board with a fine
flourish and drying her hands. 'I'll come with you since I
appear to have no choice in the matter, but I'll tell you one
thing for sure—your family will be left in no doubt whatso-

ever that I loathe, hate and detest the very sight of you!'

Having delivered her speech, she felt it a great pity she couldn't have followed through her intention of storming out to the living room and leaving him to chew on that for a while. But as she went to speed past him, she found the solidity of his form in front of her, found her arms caught in a merciless grip, and her feet barely touched the ground as he yanked her ruthlessly up against his body. She was forced to look into his face, and what she saw there had her gasping for air. His look was barbaric, and if she had any doubts that he held all the high cards, he didn't leave her in doubt for very long.

'You say just one word out of place when we get there,' he threatened, and she could see he meant it, 'and I'll have you and that precious brother of yours behind bars so fast you won't have time to wonder what's hit you!' All thought of defiance fled as she looked back at him. He looked mad enough to break her in two. 'We're going to my home to celebrate my brother's engagement. You let just one word escape those cheating lips to put a blight on those celebrations and by *God*, you'll be sorry!'

It was to be a family party then, Tully thought, her brain going round in a chaotic whirl. She couldn't think why she was to be included in the celebrations, but the menacing look Yate Meachem was favouring her with was frightening away her reasoning powers. All that was really getting through was that Richard was not out of the wood even yet and wouldn't be unless she was on her very best behaviour this weekend.

The grip on her upper arms tightened when she hadn't thought that was possible, she winced in pain as he gritted, 'Do you understand me?' and accompanied the words with a none too gentle shake.

'Yes,' was forced out of her. She wished it had come out less submissively, but she was too terrified of him to argue further.

'Good,' he said, and flung her from him so that she was glad to hang on to the table for support. 'The name is Yate,' he snarled, looking at her as though she was something that had just crawled out from under a stone and offended him. 'Use it.'

'Yes—all r-right.' She was glad to hear her voice was sounding slightly stronger, hated to think that the barely leashed violence in him had made her so cowardly, but in her defence she reasoned that to have defied him, the mood he was in, would have had those large hands of his going round her throat and squeezing the life out of her. The very thought made her swallow nervously. She still didn't feel very safe with him blocking the doorway.

Then miraculously she saw the furious look of rage leave him. 'God, but you're bloody aggravating,' he muttered, almost as if regretting he had been so rough with her. 'Did I hurt you?'

She could feel the numbness leaving her arms, only for that numbness to take possession of her thoughts that his roughness with her, now that his temper had gone, bothered him at all.

'Does it matter?' she asked huskily, and because she could no longer go on looking at him, she looked down at the tiled floor, and when next he spoke his voice had taken on that harsh cynical edge she was used to.

'You'd better go and change,' he told her. 'And for heaven's sake take your hair out of those rubber bands—my family will think I've snatched you out of the schoolroom!'

Tully reckoned she could just about cope with him in this mood and was glad to feel her courage surging back as she left the support of the kitchen table.

'They're more used to seeing you with much more sophisticated women than I am, I suppose?' she said, her spirits growing all the time.

'I'll give you this, Tully—you don't stay down for long, do you?' he replied, which was no sort of answer, she thought, though she knew anyway. His women would be all streamlined and willing bed co-habitees. She was relieved when he stepped out of the way to allow her to go past him without her having to touch him.

It was purely an act of defiance that she donned her black trouser suit. It was a great pity, she thought, that she didn't have a black sweater to go with it and complete the pitcure of mourning, but in any case it was too hot to wear a sweater beneath the jacket, and she had to admit once she had made up her eyes and put a smear of lipstick on her mouth, the whole picture was brightened and she felt she looked smart enough to meet Yate Meachem's people.

Not seeking his approval, she saw his eyes travel over her when she joined him in the living room, saw his glance go to her hair, now free from the rubber bands he had objected to and swinging clean and shining to her shoulders.

'Will I do?' she asked, purely because she was embarrassed by his scrutiny and needed to say something to get her over the moment. It was the first time he had seen her with make-up on—the first time he had seen her at all, come to that, looking anywhere near the person she really was.

For answer he moved and came close up to her. 'You'll do,' he said briefly, his voice quiet, the harshness missing. Then, when it was the last thing she was expecting, he bent his head and taking her completely by surprise, he kissed her fleetingly on the lips with a gentleness she hadn't suspected him of possessing. He straightened up, seemed to be amused for a scant second by the disbelieving look on her face, then told her, 'I'll get your case—it's time we weren't here.'

CHAPTER FIVE

CONVERSATION between them was unnecessary. What had they got to say to each other anyway that hadn't already been said? Tully was virtually his prisoner. He knew it and she was having to accept it. For herself she might yet have tried to get away, but there wasn't only herself to think of.

Yate Meachem was a good driver, she had to give him that as he effortlessly steered the car away from London. She would like to have asked which part of the world they were likely to end up in, but she hadn't spoken to him since he had kissed her back in his apartment. It seemed, she thought, a wry smile playing around her mouth, that kissing her was a far more effective way of shutting her up than any other method he had so far tried.

And what about that kiss? It had been shattering in its simplicity. If she had thought about him kissing her, and heaven knew she was putting all her energies into thinking about anything other than when that would happen, but she would have thought his kiss would be harsh like the man, ungentle, taking. But it hadn't been like that. He hadn't so much as held her with his hands, just leaned forward and bestowed that gentle kiss, almost as though he was saying, 'I'm sorry I was so rough with you.' He wasn't sorry, of course, not him, but that didn't lessen the fact that his kiss had shaken her. It had been brief, unexpected, and there hadn't been time for her to panic and wonder was this the start, for he hadn't followed it up as she would have supposed, but just stepped back from her and told her it was time they were going.

'Something amusing you?'

She hadn't known he had flicked several glances at her, hadn't known she had been smiling—she had nothing to smile about.

'No,' she said shortly, matching her tone to his. 'Maybe I'm going lightheaded under the strain.'

'Not you,' he returned. 'Your breed is as tough as old boots.'

'Thank you,' she said sweetly.

'Don't mention it.'

Some time over the weekend, she vowed, she was going to have the last word. But having found her tongue, she felt more able to ask him what she wanted to know.

'Would you tell me where we're going?' she asked, not thinking he would deign to enlighten her.

'We're making for a village on the outskirts of Oxford,' he told her. 'We should be there in about half an hour.'

'You said you had a brother—who else am I to meet?' She had visions of several brothers all looking just like him, all having the same hard unyielding manner—not her idea of a fun weekend at all.

'There'll be Jackie, Bart's fiancée, and my mother.'

Just three of them. That didn't sound too bad. Though that was three too many if she had to go through the rest of today and all tomorrow trying to keep her hate of the man by her side from showing.

'I only hope they're not too surprised at seeing me,' she said, thinking that if she tried from now to Christmas she would never appear the sophisticated type he must usually take home.

'Fishing?' He would think that wouldn't he.

'Not in the least. I merely thought your family would be surprised because I'm not the usual sort of female you bring home and because they don't in any case expect me.'

'Since you have no idea of the sort of female I take home your speculations could be way off beam,' he told her. So he did sometimes take his girl-friends there. 'And to put you right on another matter, I rang my mother this morning while you were asleep. They're expecting you all right.'

If this piece of information was meant to make her feel better, though she doubted that was his intention, then it failed miserably. For all Tully could see was that Yate Meachem meant to make her his mistress this weekend, and surely he didn't intend to do that under the same roof as his brother and mother. Her disquiet grew that that was exactly what he did intend.

'Your mother will have a room ready for me?' she tried again, definitely angling now and wondering if she could find sufficient strength to move a roomful of furniture up against the bedroom door—it wouldn't be for the want of trying if she couldn't.

She supposed she half expected the laugh that came from him at her blatant fishing. What surprised her was that the sound of his genuine laughter had a pleasant ring to it. Though she thought there was nothing at all pleasant about him or his laughter when serious once more, that harsh note returned, and he said:

'Now why should a room be prepared for you? No one will expect you to be anything other than my mistress— you'll be sharing quarters with me.'

The rest of the journey was completed in frozen silence. She had been hard put not to attack him violently with her bare hands, but checked the impulse, though only with difficulty, feeling that he was probably quite capable of driving the car one-handed, while he used the other to flatten her.

The Grange, when it came into view, made her rapidly revise her opinion that her previous circle of friends had been on a par with his. For Westover Rise, her old home, that had always seemed a vast place to her, would be lost by the side of this place. The lawns on either side of the long, long drive seemed to go on for acres and acres, and she realised then that whereas she had thought at one time she had been well off, Yate Meachem and his family must be in the millionaire class.

When he pulled up outside the front door Tully felt the greatest reluctance to move. This was it, she couldn't help thinking. This was where it all started. Then Yate was round her side of the car, his sardonic look telling her he had observed her reluctance.

'I would never have pegged you as being the shy sort,' he said, his hand coming lightly to her elbow. His light touch didn't fool her—he'd drag her from the car if she didn't make some move soon.

'You don't know the first thing about me,' she said sharply, pulling her elbow away from him and getting from the car unaided.

'I've got all weekend to find out more, then, haven't I, Tully?'

She gave him a killing look, then concentrated on looking anywhere but at him as they went up stone steps to the front door. The Grange was quite an old building, but not only was the outside in excellent repair, but if the hall was anything to go by, the inside was immaculate too. No dry rot here, she thought, remembering that Westover Rise had needed extensive work on it and how lucky they had been to get a buyer prepared to have the repairs carried out.

A small, slightly plump woman saw them as she was crossing the hall. She was dressed in a severe-looking dress, but her face suddenly broke into a softening beaming smile as she caught sight of them and hurried up to them.

'Oh, I'm so glad to see you, Mr Yate,' she said, and Tully thought had she not been there, the woman she presumed to be the housekeeper would have burst into tears.

'And I'm glad to see you, Evie,' Yate responded. And while Tully stood watching her astounded eyes saw him, entirely out of character she thought, put an arm around the woman he had called Evie and give her a hug.

'It's almost a year,' Evie said when he let her go and she stood gazing up at him, and would have said more except that Yate turned to Tully and said:

'This is Mrs Everley. She's looked after us for as long as I can remember and we're too selfish to let her retire. Evie, this is Miss Tully Vickery, a—friend of mine.'

'I'm so pleased to meet you, Miss Vickery,' said Mrs Everley, her smile extending to Tully. 'Mrs Meachem said Mr Yate was bringing his young lady to see us, and I'm so glad.'

She had obviously missed his hesitation before he had introduced her purely as 'a—friend', but her smile had warmed Tully's disconsolate spirits, and without her thinking about it her hand came out to shake hands with the housekeeper. Then because she had to say something, she found herself telling the biggest lie of all, and felt Yate's hard look on her as she said it.

'I'm pleased to be here,' she lied, and was glad she wasn't called upon to perjure her soul further, as she heard Yate asking if anyone was at home.

'Mrs Meachem is in the drawing room—she can't have heard your car or she would have come and greeted you. Mr Bart and his fiancée are out on the estate somewhere.'

'We'll go and say hello to my mother,' Yate told her. 'Can you lay some tea on, Evie? I expect Miss Vickery is dying for a cup,' and at her look that nothing would be any trouble for him, 'We'll have it upstairs in about fifteen minutes.'

Mrs Everley went to do his bidding, her step light when Tully reckoned she must be past sixty. But her thoughts then were more concerned with her lack of courage to countermand his order and say she would like to have her tea downstairs. But she consoled herself that it would be better if she didn't do anything to earn his full-scale retribution at this early stage, and anyway since it looked as if Yate could do no wrong in Mrs Everley's eyes, his were the only instructions she was going to obey anyway.

'This way.'

She was aware of his hand on her upper arm, was aware too that her arm still felt sensitive from his crushing grip on her before when he had looked set to murder her. She shrugged her arm, but he didn't let go his hold. Did he think she was going to run away or something? He led her to one of the doors along the hall, barely pausing before he opened it and urged her through.

She had only sufficient time to notice that it was a huge room yet still managed to look comfortable, when a woman with white hair got to her feet from one of the settees and started to come across the room with a joyous cry of, 'Yate!'

Yate Meachem left Tully's side, and she was struck again by the uncharacteristic and warm way he greeted his mother. 'Oh, it is good to see you here in your own home again, Yate,' and this time there were definite tears, Tully saw.

Mrs Everley had said it was almost a year since Yate had been home, yet it was only about an hour's run from London. There was some mystery here, but just then wasn't the time to try and sort out what it was, for Mrs Meachem was coming to her, extending both hands.

'So this is Tully—I'm so glad you could come,' she welcomed her. 'Yate has told me barely anything about you, so we'll have to have a chat—but I never pry, so please don't think I'm the prying sort.'

'Of course not,' Tully said automatically, liking this woman immediately. She had all the warmth in her that Yate Meachem lacked. Perhaps her other son, Bart, had been blessed with Yate's share.

'I'm afraid you'll have to leave getting to know Tully until later,' Yate was saying when Tully had dried up because though she wanted to return the warmth Mrs Meachem was extending, it came to her how entirely false was her position in this household this weekend. And having met Yate's mother, she found she just couldn't show her the hate she had spoken of showing for her son. This woman would be entirely bewildered by it, she saw, and not only that, Mrs Meachem was almost over the moon that Yate had come home at all.

'Oh?' Mrs Meachem enquired, as though she, like Tully, was wondering what was coming.

'Tully barely had any sleep last night,' Yate explained. 'If she's not going to nod off in the middle of tonight's celebrations, I think it would be a good idea if she rested from now until dinner.'

Tully's jaw very nearly dropped at this. To anyone who didn't know differently, it would sound as though Yate regarded her as something to be cherished. From the more than understanding look in his mother's eyes, Mrs Meachem certainly thought so, but Tully's disquiet was growing by the minute, wondering what he was up to now.

'You had a late night?' Mrs Meachem enquired.

'Dawn had broken before Tully closed her eyes,' Yate said smoothly, and Tully couldn't argue against that. 'And she was in my kitchen at eleven,' he added, unnecessarily, she thought. His mother would think she couldn't leave him alone.

'Oh,' Mrs Meachem said softly, as if seeing all her son was telling her and far more. Whatever her conclusions, from the look on her face she couldn't have been more pleased, Tully thought. 'You must be exhausted, my dear,' she said, turning to her, then back to her son. 'Everything is ready for you, Yate, just as you asked. Shall I ask Evie to bring some tea up? I expect you could both do with some.'

One emotion after another was shooting through Tully as Yate told his mother he had already seen Evie and asked her about tea. Mrs Meachem, she thought, was taking it very matter-of-factly that her son should bring home a girl she had never met before, and within minutes she had suggested they go upstairs. Mrs Meachem hadn't so much as batted an eyelid that they were to share the same room, indeed she had actually seconded Yate's opinion that tea in that same room was a good idea.

Embarrassed colour flooded through her cheeks though she was aware that she was the only one in the room to feel any embarrassment. She knew Yate had witnessed her heightened colour from the way he turned her from his mother's view and said softly, and to her astonished ears, in a voice that sounded perfectly normal—it would to his mother at any rate:

'Come on, Tully, it's bed for you.'

Tully couldn't get out of the drawing room quickly enough. Oh, heavens, the whole charade was a nightmare! Didn't anyone have morals any more? Yet she could have sworn from her first impression of his mother that she wouldn't countenance her son taking a house guest to bed in the afternoon. *Bed in the afternoon!* Panic streaked through her, and her feet stood rooted to the carpet, then she felt the hard pressure of Yate's arm around her waist and knew he was ready to propel her forcibly from the room, heard him telling his mother, 'Tully's dead on her feet—I'll be down later.' Tully feeling that iron clamp at the back of her knew then if she didn't move her feet towards that door, he would not hesitate to pick her up and carry her. He was big enough to do it too, and cover his action with some joking remark for his mother's benefit.

Her head came up, and with all the dignity she could muster she went with him. His arm dropped from her waist once they were outside the door, and not wanting him to touch her again, she stepped smartly away towards the staircase.

'Not that way,' his voice stopped her, and she turned, but had no time to wonder, what now? for he was saying, 'We're in the west wing,' and escorting her to the far end of the hall, away from the main staircase to the foot of another narrower stairway.

Without looking at him, she began to ascend the stairs. She wouldn't speak to him either, she would save all her energies for the battle that was likely to commence any moment at all now. But she received the shock of her life when, gaining the head of the stairs, Yate stepped past her and opened one of the many doors there, and stood back to allow her to precede him into what she had been convinced would be a bedroom.

Only it wasn't a bedroom, but a well furnished sitting room, and there pulled up in front of a deep and wide settee was a low table holding a tea tray complete with the most delicate china cups she had ever seen.

'Oh!' escaped her.

He didn't pretend he didn't know what her 'Oh!' had been about. 'The bedroom's through there,' he said, pointing to the only other door in the room, and then coolly, 'Will you be mother?'

Unspeaking Tully went to the settee and sat down. Truth to tell, she hadn't noticed before Yate had mentioned it how very tired she was, but it came home to her now, and she hoped a reviving cup of tea would give her the strength she would need to try and get Yate to change his mind about the plans he had for her.

'Sugar?' She had poured two cups, and her instinct had been to push the sugar bowl across so he could help himself, but on second thoughts if she was to appeal to anything civilised in him, she thought it might help if she began acting a little civilised herself.

'Two, please,' he said, and sat back on the settee beside her, seeming content to sit and wait for her to perform this everyday courtesy.

Careful not to slop any of his tea in his saucer, though her fingers were visibly trembling, Tully handed him his cup. She was aware that he hadn't taken his eyes off her the whole time, and cleared her throat nervously, knowing the time for putting off this discussion would be too late once he had drunk his tea.

'Mr Meachem——' she saw his brows come down, realised she had made her first blunder before she had even got started, and tried again. 'Y-Yate,' she said, calling him by his forename for the first time. 'Yate, I—that is—well, you aren't really m-meaning to carry this thing through, are you?'

'What thing would this be, Tully?'

Damn him, he could see she was nervous. He knew full well what she was talking about. 'Th-this mistress thing—you know what I mean.'

'Are you saying at this late stage that bed with me has no appeal for you?'

Her first impression of him had been right, he was a swine, a perfect swine. 'Damn you, Yate Meachem, you know it hasn't!'

'But you agreed, Tully—don't you remember? If I didn't report you to the police,' he pointed out reasonably, 'you agreed to be my bed partner.'

'I didn't agree to any such thing,' she said hotly, and had to place her cup and saucer down on the tray before in her agitation it slopped all over her.

'You would rather that I called the police—that I had them investigate, had them discover how you happened to have your brother's keys in your possession?'

That harsh note was back in his voice. She'd had a suspicion he had been merely playing with her before, but he wasn't playing now. And at the mention of her brother Tully smelt the acrid smell of full defeat and knew at that moment she could say goodbye to any ideas she might have had of marrying Howard.

With the air of one who, if medicine had to be taken, would rather take it all in one go, take it quickly now and be done with it, Tully raised her head, her outward expression as defeated as she was inwardly feeling. Hard unfriendly blue eyes looked back at her and she couldn't take any more. She only hoped her fighting spirit would stay down, that she wouldn't fight him all the way when the time came. At least let her come out of this with some of her dignity intact—she closed her eyes.

'Would you do—what you have to do now, please,' she said, resignation in every weary syllable. 'I'd like to get it over with as quickly as possible.'

She waited, her heart going like a faulty outboard motor. She was sure it would stop altogether if he didn't make some move soon. She expected his arms to come out and grab her, for his mouth to suffocate hers with kisses, but when after an agony of waiting he hadn't moved, she opened her eyes and it was to look directly into his, to see him leaning back against one corner of the settee, his hands nowhere near her but resting loosely on his well muscled thighs. And then, the most enraging, final humiliation of all—he opened his mouth and burst out laughing.

He was actually laughing, laughing *at her*! He could have no idea what it had cost her to offer herself the way she had done, he had no idea of how cheap and completely degraded she felt, and just to loll there casually, and laugh. Both her hands came up together, and with all her might she struck him first on one cheek and went to hit him on the other.

Her hand was gripped in a vicelike hold before her second blow could reach him, but she was unrepentant. 'Now laugh!' she yelled at him. 'You ... you ...' and then what she had been dreading all along had come about, for he moved with lightning speed, was relaxed and casual no longer, and she was physically lifted until she was lying across him.

'That's more like it—Now, my sacrificial lamb ...' she heard him say between gritted teeth, '*now*!'

She understood then, understood too late, as his mouth came down ruthlessly on hers, that Yate Meachem would never have touched her while she offered herself in that submissive way. He was, as every instinct had told her, only she had turned her back on that instinct, he was a man who liked to fight for what he wanted, enjoyed the hunt, and by the very way she had attacked him she had set light to that all male urge to be the hunter.

But even knowing that, her moment of weakness over, her moment of submission gone as she fought with everything in her while his mouth took what he wanted from her mouth, she realised that never had she been kissed like this before. Howard's kisses had been watery by comparison. Thoughts of Howard were growing dim, but she renewed her fight as Yate's mouth left hers and sought and found the hollows in her throat, his hands coming to undo the button on the jacket of her trouser suit.

Her cry, 'No!' rent the air more than once, and as she became aware that he was slipping her jacket from her shoulders, her efforts took on a frenzied fury. 'No!' she screamed again, trying to pull her jacket back on to her shoulders and knowing there was no one to hear her, isolated as they were in the west wing. 'No,' she said again, as his hands pushed hers away from her jacket and he slipped the straps of her bra down her arms. 'No, Yate, don't!'

Her entreaties were useless, as she found herself lying down on the settee with Yate partly on top of her, his body pressing in to her. Then once more his mouth found hers, forcing her lips apart as he ransacked the delights her mouth had to offer.

Just when exhaustion overcame her fear Tully didn't know. She was aware that the strength of her grip on his wrist as his hand would have touched her breast was flagging. Somewhere at the back of her mind she was vaguely aware that he was barely exerting a quarter of his strength, just using enough to quell her rebellious spirit but no more. Her hand dropped away from his wrist and she knew that at any time the hand that hovered could have touched her swelling contours. But surprisingly it didn't. She opened her eyes, exhaustion and shock wide in the depths of her velvety brown eyes.

'Please don't, Yate,' she said, and this time her voice was quiet, for the moment defeated.

Not quite believing it, she felt and saw him roll away from her, experienced fresh alarm when she looked down and saw that though her lacy bra was still covering her, there was much too much of her showing. Her colour high, she watched, not really believing any of this was happening to her, saw he was pushing her bra straps back into place, pulling her jacket back on to her shoulders, then without a word he was picking her up and holding her in his arms.

Fear showed in her eyes as she looked into blue eyes that had a warmer light in them now. Yate took a step away from the settee. 'Where are you going with me?' It came out quickly for all she felt all the fight had gone out of her; she didn't know where she was going to get the strength to resist if he was still set on making her his.

'You're going to bed,' he said quietly, and as she began to struggle, he held her firmly and added, 'You're worn out—you're going to sleep—alone.'

Feeling she had awakened from someone else's nightmare, Tully was stiff in his arms as he carried her through to the bedroom and placed her on the bed. Her eyes looked back at him, wary, not trusting. Then as he stood there meeting her suspicious look he sat down on the bed beside her.

'I'd take you out of your trouser suit myself, Tully,' he told her, 'but I'm sure you'd suspect my motives. Get out of it as soon as I've gone, there's a good girl.' And then, as he had done once before, he lowered his head and gently touched her mouth with his, then left her.

Wondering if she was doing the right thing, not at all sure he wouldn't return, but too exhausted to care any more, Tully tiredly got out of her suit, climbed in between the covers of the big double bed, and while her mind was still cogitating on what had happened, she fell asleep.

She came up from the depths of sleep to hear a maid gently calling her awake. Seeing the girl who had looked so beautiful in sleep was even more beautiful with her eyes open, the shy young girl revealed that her name was Marian, and also told Tully that dinner was to be served in an hour but that the family would like her to join them in the drawing room for a pre-dinner drink.

'Mr Yate said he thought it would save time if I unpacked for you,' Marian added.

About to refuse, Tully saw that Yate was right. The request that she join them for a pre-dinner drink was an order, she saw that too, and since she didn't want him anywhere near her while she was getting ready, she realised it would be better to do as he commanded.

'Would you mind—have you the time to spare?' she asked Marian, smiling genuinely in an effort to get the younger girl to lose her shyness.

'Oh yes,' Marian said eagerly, already on her knees and opening the case she had probably brought in with her, Tully thought, since it hadn't been there when she had gone to sleep.

She hoped it *was* Marian who had brought in her case, but it could have been Yate, she supposed, though she didn't like the idea of him coming in and looking at her while she was asleep. He had done that before, she recalled; he must have done, for no one else could have pulled that blanket over her as she lay sleeping on the settee in his apartment. That was out of character too, she mused, before coming to the conclusion that she knew little about him anyway. More often than not he was brutal to her—took delight in half frightening her to death, and yet twice, each time when he had been particularly cruel to her, he had given her that gentle kiss, almost as if he was saying sorry.

Tully forced him out of her mind and got out of bed. After tomorrow, thank goodness, she would never see him again. Oh, how she was counting the hours! Seeing Marian had placed her robe at the foot of the bed, she shrugged into it and noticed her surroundings. It came to her as she looked around that though the furniture looked old and well cared for, the walls, curtain and carpets gave the room an unused look. The paintwork was immaculate, not a chip or a blemish anywhere, though if it had been recently decorated she could detect no smell of paint.

It was funny, she thought, how one noticed inconsequential things when one's whole mind was a quagmire of torment. She saw another door in the room opposite to the door Yate had carried her through and walked over to it hoping it was the bathroom. She could have asked Marian where the bathroom was, she supposed, but heaven alone knew what the young girl thought already of the goings on at the Grange.

It was a bathroom, and looking as new and as pristine as the room she had slept in. The bath hadn't been used, she saw as she turned on the taps, having expected to find it a little damp if Yate was already dressed and downstairs. Where had he changed? She'd have heard him, surely, if he had changed in the bedroom? But she mustn't think about him, she must hurry. There was no saying he wouldn't come looking for her. But having decided to put him out of her mind, she couldn't help but wonder that, the advantages all his, he had dropped her on the bed and left her.

Marian was nowhere to be seen when Tully, fully refreshed from her bath, hurried into the bedroom. Seated before the dressing table, she paid extra attention to her eyes; her skin was pure and clean and needed no more than a dab of powder to take the shine from her bath away. A light application of lipstick, her hair brushed into shining waves and left to flow freely to her shoulders— now to get into her clothes. She had packed only one dress that could be called partyish, had secretly hoped that she might be wearing it to celebrate her own engagement, but there was no time to dwell on that now. Half expecting to find Yate's clothes hanging beside hers, Tully opened the wardrobe door and seeing only her own belongings, opened the other door thinking his things must be on the other side, but no, there were only her clothes hanging there. Her brow crinkled in thought as she pondered the absence of his possessions until she worked out that of course, with her asleep, someone would probably unpack for him later. She moved her things up to make room for his, unconscious that she was assisting him rather than obstructing.

The midnight blue dress suited her, she thought, its thin straps showing her creamy shoulders to advantage, the single layer of chiffon covering the fine material beneath definitely giving her a dainty feminine look even though she didn't think five foot seven could be called dainty. Yes, she would do, she thought, as she twisted round to get a side view.

A gasp escaped her as she studied her reflection in the mirror. No wonder her arms where Yate had gripped her this morning felt sensitive to touch! The backs of her arms were covered in bruises—she couldn't go anywhere dressed like this.

The door opened while she was still meditating what to do. Her eyes flew to see Yate standing there, big, powerful, essentially male and looking if not exactly handsome, then extremely distinguished in his dinner clothes. For no reason Tully felt her heart turn over as she stood staring wordlessly at him. He was the first to speak, and if she had thought she had seen a glimpse of admiration there as his eyes slowly travelled over her, there was none of that admiration there when he said coolly:

'We're waiting for you.'

'I can't come.'

The words had left her without thought. She saw his eyes harden and knew she wasn't going to get away without a very good explanation. But since he wanted her decked out in a party dress and it wasn't possible to wear the only one she had with her ...

'I warn you, Tully, I'm in no mood for games.' She had an idea then that something else besides her had upset him.

'I'm not playing games,' she said, and was suddenly oddly reluctant to show him her bruises though it was he who had caused them. 'This dress isn't suitable after all,' and as it looked as though he was about to contradict her, 'and I don't have another more suitable dress with me.'

She'd been stupid to think he would accept what she told him without question. Though perhaps he sensed she wasn't being so straightforward with him as he was used to, for his voice was quite mild when he asked, 'Perhaps you'll tell me what exactly is wrong with your dress. From where I'm standing you look very—presentable.'

With a resigned sigh she turned her back to him. 'My arms,' she said quietly. 'I've only just noticed.'

'Good God!' the voice sounded strangled somehow before a firmer note crept into it. 'Did I do that to you?'

She felt him move and flinched as his hands came down on her shoulders, but he didn't let go his hold of her as he turned her round to face him. What she should have done, of course, was to have glared at him accusingly. But something, she wasn't sure what, was reaching her from him. Something was telling her he was regretting being the one to have treated her so. Tully couldn't look at him, and then she felt his hand come beneath her chin, forcing her head up, making her look at him. The hardness, she saw, had gone.

'I'm wondering, Tallulah Vickery,' he said softly, 'which of us is the bigger villain—you with your sticky fingers or me with my flesh bruisers.'

At his reference to her sticky fingers, any momentary weakening on her side fell away. 'Far be it from me to call you the big bully you know you are!' she snapped, and was ready for all-out warfare, only to have him take the wind out of her sails as he had the power to do time and time again, this time by ignoring that she seemed ready for a fight.

'Let's have a look and see what else you've brought with you.' Tully knew then that if he had to dress her in jeans and a parka he would insist she accompany him downstairs. Though why, she couldn't begin to guess.

CHAPTER SIX

STRANGELY, Tully was glad of Yate's arm around her waist as they crossed the hall towards the drawing room. It gave her confidence a boost, though she had never thought her confidence to be lacking before. It was this dress, she supposed. Everyone else would be dressed to kill, and here was she in an ankle-length dress that although entirely suitable for dinner with its long flowing sleeves, was all of two years old. She had bought it just before Monty had died, had found it irresistible then with its square neck cut narrowly at the shoulders to reveal a goodly expanse of her creamy skin, but there was nothing about it that could be called a party dress.

Yate halted with her just outside the drawing room, and she looked up questioningly. 'Tully Vickery is looking beautiful,' he said, and dropped a light kiss on the end of her nose, then opened the door and pushed her through.

A smile curved her lips as she stood just inside the room. Only moments ago she had never felt less like smiling, and it shook her somewhat that that absurd remark and brief salute from the man she hated should make her feel this way, as if it didn't matter a jot if she had come to this party dressed in a nylon overall.

'Ah, Yate—Tully,' Mrs Meachem smiled at them as Yate, his arm round Tully's waist, once more urged her forward.

He didn't apologise for being late, and Tully's apology was taken from her as she saw that besides Mrs Meachem there were only two other people in the room, a pleasant-featured blonde girl a few years older than herself, and a man with the same fair hair as Yate and looking to be three or four years younger. But whether he was as tall as Yate she couldn't tell, for he was sitting in a wheelchair.

'Come and say hello to Jackie and Bart,' Yate was saying, and Tully wasn't feeling like smiling any more. Her natural good manners she hoped had kept Bart from seeing how shocked she was to see him wheelchair-bound, but Yate should have told her.

There was tension in the air. Tully could feel it, and knew it didn't all emanate from her, for apart from Yate these other people had done nothing for her to get strung up about. Jackie, extending her hand, broke the sudden tension.

'How do you do, Tully,' she said, and if she had felt the tension too it wasn't apparent in her open smile. 'We're so glad you were able to come with Yate today—it's nice to have all the family together.'

Tully smiled back, her own hand coming out automatically. Was Jackie in effect saying that if she hadn't come with Yate, he wouldn't have come at all? she wondered incredulously. But before she could say anything, she became aware that Bart Meachem was studying her. His look seemed to be saying a cynical, 'So you're Yate's latest', and she couldn't tell from his look whether or not he approved. That tension was there again. She looked from Bart to Jackie, saw that Jackie was nibbling away at her bottom lip as if fearful of something, but of what Tully had no idea. And then, as she looked at Jackie, she remembered that this should be one of the happiest days of her life, though there wasn't much evidence of that from the way the girl was hovering uncertainly by as though unsure of Bart's mood, and Tully with the sensitivity that was part and parcel of her nature suddenly saw that somehow or other whether the evening was a success or not seemed to have something to do with her being there. She held out her hand to Bart and said mischievously:

'Yate should have told me—you're better looking than he is.'

As though by magic the tension seemed to lift. Everybody laughed, even Yate, she noticed from the corner of her eye.

'And Yate should have told me that Miss Tully Vickery is something of a charmer,' said Bart, grinning at her and extending his hand.

Tully forgot after that that she was here solely as Yate's prisoner. Two other couples joined them for dinner, aunts and uncles of Yate and Bart, and after dinner several friends of Jackie and Bart arrived and they all adjourned to one of the rooms where the carpet had been taken up to allow for dancing.

Jackie and Bart seemed to be admirably suited, Tully thought, and though she couldn't help noticing that Yate and Bart barely exchanged half a dozen words with each other, the evening seemed to be going with a swing. What did surprise her, though, was the way that Yate rarely left her side. Though on thinking about it, she realised with a sinking feeling that he was taking no chances with her, if she had changed her safe-cracking habits to those of pick-pocket.

'What's the matter?' Yate was again at her side, having just spent a few brief minutes in conversation with his uncle.

'Matter?'

'What's upset you? You were sparkling when I left you.' Then remembering she had been in a group with his brother at that time, 'Bart hasn't been being disagreeable, has he?'

Disagreeable? Bart? Already she had noticed that there didn't seem to be any love lost between the two brothers, and it came to her then that if Yate thought Bart had been rude to her and took exception to it, though she couldn't think that anyone's rudeness to her would bother him one whit, then if the breach between him and Bart wasn't to be widened still further she was going to have to confess what she had been thinking about.

'Bart has been a perfect gentleman,' she said, hoping to get away with leaving it at that, only to receive one of Yate's looks that said, 'I'm waiting.' Knowing patience wasn't his greatest virtue—she had yet to find anything that was—she told him frankly, 'I've just realised why you've been shadowing me all evening.'

'Oh?' There was an alert look in his eyes that told her he knew what she was talking about. Since he already knew, she found it a little disconcerting when he said, 'Perhaps you'd like to explain that remark?'

Without looking at him Tully said, 'I know you don't trust me, but I—hadn't supposed you would bring me into your home and then watch every move I make.'

'Every move you make?' he queried, just as though he didn't know what she was talking about, she thought.

'I give you my word I won't go round stealing wallets or pinching the splendid array of diamonds I see worn here tonight,' she told him dully, and felt again the same remembered urge to hit him when he burst out laughing. His laughter attracted Bart's look and she saw Bart look at his brother and smile. And that confused her further, for Bart's smile had been one of pleasure at seeing his brother laughing, supposedly happily, and she had rapidly then to revise her opinion that there was little love lost between the brothers.

'You've got it all wrong, Tully.' Yate's laughter had gone from him, but she was still niggled by it and in no mood to believe him.

'I'm sure I have,' she answered sweetly, but he didn't enlighten her on where she had got it all wrong.

'Come on, dance with me,' he said, and because he wasn't

asking but telling her, she went with him, felt his arms come round her, and with wonder found herself being charmed out of her irritation with him, so that by the time the music ended and they left the floor she was on the point of letting herself be amused by something he had said.

The aunts and uncles were the first to leave, and then gradually the others trickled away until there was just the five of them left.

'Shall we return to the drawing room?' Yate suggested. 'A nightcap, I think, then bed.'

'Well, I really enjoyed the evening,' Mrs Meachem said once they all, with the exception of Yate who was dispensing drinks, were sitting down. 'What do you think, Bart—were you pleased with everything?'

'Everything,' Bart agreed with some satisfaction. Yate was just handing Tully her champagne and as she looked up to thank him, she saw from the look on his face at Bart's comment that he too looked well pleased.

After Yate had satisfied himself that everyone had a drink he came and sat beside Tully on the settee. 'Did you enjoy yourself?' he enquired, his voice low, making it look to anyone watching as though his words were for her alone.

'Yes, thank you,' Tully said primly, not sure why she was receiving this personal attention but having a fair idea it was a prelude of things to come. Champagne tumbled over the rim of her glass as her fingers began to shake uncontrollably.

'Careful, darling,' Yate shattered her by saying, which did nothing for her tightening nerves. She looked away from him and saw three pairs of eyes were looking at them.

'That's wedding march talk,' Bart addressed his brother, referring to the endearment he had uttered as though he was unused to his brother being so openly demonstrative.

'A slip of the tongue,' Yate parried. 'No more than that, I promise you,' he joked. But Tully had the strangest idea then that that 'darling' had been trotted out deliberately. And on top of that, she had the clearest conviction that for some reason or another Yate Meachem was using her entirely for his own ends, and those ends had very little to do with the fact that he had stated he wanted a mistress for this weekend.

She contributed very little to the conversation after that, but quite enjoyed listening to what the others had to say. Though it was Mrs Meachem who seemed to do most of the talking, seeming as far as Tully could make out, determined to say something at every sentence which would mean Yate and Bart would have to get into conversation with each other. Jackie too, as far as she could see, seemed to encourage this, but apart from the occasional surface remark, both brothers had little to say. And it was Yate who was the first to indicate that the evening had gone on for long enough.

With sickening dread Tully heard him say, 'Well, I'm for bed—coming, Tully?'

She knew she was blushing as she got to her feet to wish them all goodnight. What were they thinking? she wondered. Then as she found herself outside the door with Yate, all thoughts of anyone else went from her, and again she was beset by the terrifying thought, was this it? Was this when it would begin?

Yate went with her into the sitting room of the small apartment in the west wing, and her nerves stretched tautly. She was afraid to say anything that might trigger off his sexual appetite, and wondered how to avoid sharing the bed in the other room with him. But it seemed that he wasn't all that eager to get into bed now that they were here and the veneer of charm that had been in evidence downstairs hadn't lasted much beyond the first tread on the staircase.

'I'm going to read for a while,' he told her, his eyes going over her, drooping now that she had no longer to put on an act. 'You'd better go to bed, you look done in.'

As a compliment it wasn't one. She gathered from that that Tully Vickery was no longer looking beautiful, but she hesitated. It didn't sound as though he meant to join her, but she was unsure, unsure what he had in mind when his reading was done. She would like to think he was the sort who never put a book down until he had finished it and that he had just started reading Tolstoy's *War and Peace*, but ...

'For the Lord's sake go to bed!' She caught his hard-eyed look on her and wanted to thump him that she apparently was the only one he ever lost patience with—there had been no sign of impatience in him downstairs. 'You're hovering about like some light forlorn moth who's lost its sense of direction.'

It was very satisfying, if childish, to slam the bedroom door shut behind her. What an almighty swine he was! It hadn't occurred to him that she had swung from one cliff's edge to another this last twenty-hour hours. Tully simmered down as she rinsed her face and changed into one of her nightdresses. It was a pity she had brought none but her prettiest nighties with her. Not that she had anticipated Howard paying her a night-time visit, she hadn't, but it was just part of the holiday spirit that had made her put in this sheer nightdress with its over-layer of delicate lace.

She had almost made it into bed when she stubbed her toe painfully, muffled the cry of momentary agony that rushed to her lips, hopped a semi-circle on one foot, lost her balance and went crashing over, taking a small chair with her.

'What the ...?'

It had been too much to hope Yate hadn't heard the re-sounding crash. For the first time she was fleetingly glad they were isolated up here and none of the staff or anyone else would be disturbed by the noise. But as she looked up, she saw Yate standing there, the absence of his jacket in no way minimising the breadth of his shoulders, and her gladness quickly evaporated.

'I stubbed my toe,' she said woefully, and because it sounded so much like a ten-year-old asking to be kissed better, she forgot she was dressed only in her enhancing nightie, and grinned unaffectedly at him. Her grin faded as she saw from his face that he could see nothing remotely funny. Badly wanting to poke her tongue out at him and cross her eyes, Tully struggled to her feet, not ready to let his glowering expression defeat her. 'Sorry to have disturbed you,' her voice was pure sugar. 'I do hope you hadn't got to the good bit.'

'Your cheeky little tongue will get you into a load of trouble one of these days,' Yate forecast, coming over to her when she no longer needed his help since she had managed to get to her feet without his assistance.

'More trouble than I'm in at the moment, you mean.' She couldn't see it herself, never again would she take the risk she had taken for Richard.

'Your troubles haven't started yet.' If he had been looking for a sure way to curb her over-active tongue, Tully was of the opinion he need look no further.

'You're reading,' she said hurriedly, backing away from him, having no trouble in following his meaning.

'My book is beginning to bore me.'

Oh dear, she didn't like the turn this conversation was taking one little bit. 'Perhaps it will pick up,' she said bravely, wanting badly to hide herself beneath the bed covers but suddenly terrified of going anywhere near that bed.

'Maybe it won't,' Yate answered, coming nearer.

'H-have you read *Jonathan Livingston Seagull* by Richard Bach? I f-found it extremely good,' said Tully, clutching at straws and coming up against the wall as she took yet another step backwards.

'Oh, Tully, you slay me,' said Yate with a short laugh, but his laughter didn't stop him advancing further towards her. 'I never in my life thought the day would ever come when I had a briefly clad, beautiful girl, plus a bed all in the same room, and would be party to a discussion on books I've read. But,' he had reached her, his hands came to rest on her shoulders, 'as I remember it, Jonathan found there was nothing he couldn't do once he'd put his mind to it—and now, Tully Vickery, I think the time has come for me to put my mind to silencing you by kissing those tantalising lips of yours.'

Had her toe not still been throbbing, Tully felt sure, since her arms were suddenly fastened to her sides as Yate pulled her into his arms, she would have kicked out at him, forgetting completely that she still had one uninjured foot. But as his head came down and his lips met hers in a brief unseeking kiss, she forgot she intended to fight him all the way the very next time he tried his hand at seduction, and could only stand there in the circle of his arms and stare blankly at him when he lifted his head and looked deeply into her bemused wide brown eyes.

'You have a delightful mouth, Tully,' he said softly, and while what he had said was still sinking in, he lowered his head and bestowed another unforceful kiss on her mouth, a gentle kiss that lasted a few seconds longer than the one before, then he raised his head and looked at her once more.

'I ... I ...' Tully struggled to get some words out, anything to try and put an end to this, but something was happening to her—she wanted to feel the touch of his mouth on hers again. Everything in her was telling her she should be struggling against him, kicking, biting, scratching, but her mind refused to be obeyed.

'Shh!' Yate breathed, and holding her with one arm laid a quieting finger against her lips, only to remove it to place his mouth once again gently, where his finger had been.

Of their own volition Tully's lips parted, she felt the pressure of Yate's mouth against hers increase slightly, felt the heat of his body through the thin material of her nightdress and wanted to press herself up against him. She couldn't do that, of course, her brain was telling her she couldn't and that part of her brain she took notice of, but when she felt the hard wall behind her come once more into contact with her shoulder blades as Yate moved a small pace with her and she felt her body being pressed to his, something deep inside of her ignored all common sense. She felt his hands unhurriedly on her hips, drawing her yet closer to him, knew her heart was pounding so much it threatened to jump out of her body as she felt his all-maleness against her. Vaguely the thought came that he might be seducing her then as his kiss subtly changed from being gentle to being seeking, then demanding—she couldn't doubt it, she was being seduced, and being secured by an expert.

When she had thought his kiss would never end, didn't want it to end, and Yate pulled away from her, she was all at sea. He had awoken an urgent need within her, but it looked as though that need was going to be unquenched. She hardly understood what was happening to her as she gazed back at him, her look begging him to stay, not to go away and leave her like this.

The corners of Yate's mouth lifted in a gentle smile, no mockery at all there as he asked quietly, 'All right?' She wasn't sure what he meant by that—did he mean Are you all right? Perhaps she had grown pale, though her whole body felt on fire, or perhaps he was asking permission whether to go or stay, though she would never have thought he would ask anyone's permission about anything.

'All right,' she answered, but not sure what to. All she knew was that for a while at least, she didn't want him to go.

She should have panicked, she thought, when he picked her up and carried her to the bed. But there was no panic in her, only an aching need to be kissed again as Yate lowered her down on to the bed and stretched out beside her. Somehow his shirt was undone, there was dark hair on his chest, and as his lips wandered to her eyes, to her nose, and then satisfyingly to her yearning mouth, Tully's hand found its way inside his shirt, glorying that the beat of his heart was as energetic as hers.

Effortlessly he slid her nightdress from her shoulders, his mouth and hands caressing their creamy curve. The tiny pearl buttons down the centre of her nightdress were no hindrance either as with his mouth draining, yet giving, every last bit of satisfaction from hers the first half dozen buttons slipped their moorings and his hand which had so far left her breasts untouched eased beneath the soft material. Her breath stopped on a heightened moment of anticipation while his hand seemed to linger above her, then with his mouth once more claiming her she felt a joyous surge of pleasure as the first male hand touched the naked swell of her.

'Oh, Yate,' she murmured, her pleasure at his touch causing her to arch her body to his.

His mouth left hers and he raised his head to look deep into her eyes. She saw the raging desire in his look while with his eyes still holding hers, she felt the material of her nightie being pushed to one side to uncover her breasts. Colour surged through her face that he meant to look at her, and her hand came up in shyness to the side of his face so that he should not look and feast his eyes on her nakedness. Whether he read her shyness or not she did not know, but he took hold of her hand, gentle in his, and placed a kiss in its palm before looking once more into her eyes.

'No, Yate,' she said huskily, her first protest in all that had gone before.

He seemed puzzled by her attitude. 'No?' he queried.

'I don't want you to look at me,' she said, and hoped he would understand. Would understand her shyness and forgive her for it, continue to instruct her in the ways of love without any of the aggression she knew was in him coming to the fore.

For agonising seconds it seemed, all movement from him ceased, then some of that aggression she had feared was in his voice when he said accusingly, 'I do hope, Tully Vickery, that at this late stage you're not giving me a stop signal.'

'I . . . It—isn't that.' Oh God, that not-felt-before upsurge of joy when she had been in his arms was plummeting rapidly into a never-experienced-before misery.

She knew he was fighting hard to keep his patience with her. 'Perhaps you would tell me, if it isn't a stop sign, what the hell it is?'

At the tone in his voice, Tully wanted to cover herself up, wanted him to leave her, dreaded his going, but he was pinning her down with his body and she couldn't move.

'Perhaps,' he said, his voice loaded with sarcasm, 'you've just thought of dear Howard. You're a peculiar girl, Tully Vickery. I hadn't thought, knowing what I know about you, that coming metaphorically from Howard's bed into mine would bother you.'

It came to her then, along with a shaming rush of other thoughts, that she hadn't given Howard a thought all evening, and certainly not since Yate had come into this room. It came to her that of course Yate wouldn't know her shyness for what it was; he had been fully convinced she and Howard had been to bed together.

'I ... I've never been to bed with Howard,' she stated, when she had no intention of telling him anything about her relationship with Howard.

'Never?' The word was said disbelievingly until he looked into her face and appeared to see for the first time, as her eyes could not meet his, that her avoidance of his eyes was not because she was lying, but because she was growing more and more embarrassed by the second at this new situation she found herself in. 'Good God!' seemed to be jerked from him, as though he still didn't believe it. 'You're telling me that not once have you gone to bed with this chap you're thinking of marrying?'

If Yate Meachem said, as she was sure was in his mind, 'What's wrong with the fellow,' she was going to hit him, she was sure of it, and hang the consequences.

'You've spent the night alone at his flat with him, though, haven't you?' he asked when she hadn't answered his previous question. Tully remembered that that was where she had told Richard she was spending the night and he hadn't sounded at all as though he thought that was unusual. She knew Yate was thinking if she had spent a night alone with Howard then he didn't believe that night had been spent without Howard touching her.

'The only man outside my family with whom I've spent the night has been you,' she snapped, thinking to let him see she had come through last night untouched so he needn't start scoffing at Howard's lack of ardour.

Yate moved his body away from her, and she felt cold suddenly, where minutes earlier her whole being had been aflame. 'You mean,' he said slowly, as though it was being dragged from him, 'that no man has ever touched you?— That you're a virgin?'

Scarlet colour rioted through her face again, but he re-

fused to let her look away from him as he witnessed it.
'Yes,' she whispered, and for the first time in her life
hated the fact that she was. She wanted to experience that
rapture again that had been between her and Yate—and
more. But contrary to her previous opinion that he would
relish taking a virgin to bed, the conviction was steadily
growing that he would have no use for her untried body.

'That maidenly display just now,' Yate said, and she knew
what he meant without him explaining. 'Was that because
no man has—looked at you before?'

'Y-yes.' It was barely audible, but he heard it. Then
before she knew what he was about, he gave her one long
hard look.

'Allow me to be the first,' he said, and while a fire lit
in her cheeks, his mouth tightened, then deliberately he
turned his eyes to where his hands had uncovered. Then
as though unable to prevent himself, he lowered his head
and saluted each rose-crowned summit with a kiss. 'That's
the least you owe me,' he said before turning the folds of
her nightdress to cover her—she noticed his hands did
not linger to refasten the buttons. Then getting off the
bed, he surveyed the shattered look of her. 'Might I suggest, Miss Vickery,' he said coolly, 'that the next time you
travel the road we've just ambled along, you inform your
fellow traveller at the outset that there's a halt sign not too
far along the way.'

Halt sign! Tully thought as the door closed soundlessly
behind him. She hadn't put that halt sign there, heaven
help her. He had done that. And ambled along, he had
said? She had gone galloping along scarcely knowing what
she was doing in her eagerness to get to the other end.

Shame such as she had never before known washed over
her. If only she could fall asleep perhaps she would get
some peace from her spinning thoughts. Heaven help her—
far from fighting every scrap of the way when Yate had
set about seducing her, set about fulfilling the threat that

had been hanging over her ever since he had caught her, as he thought, robbing his safe last night, she had been ready to give in without lifting one finger in protest. Oh dear heaven, how on earth was she going to face him again? He had spurned all she had to offer him, and what must he now be thinking of her? That for all her previous protests, the seduction of Tully Vickery had been too easy for him to want to proceed once he had seen she was his for the taking.

For a while she tried to place all the blame at his door, but in the end an innate deep-down fairness reared its unwanted head, and she was forced to face squarely that as soon as he had awakened desire inside her she had been unaware of existing, she had been lost. When he had given her all the time she needed to say no—she recalled the moment when he had said, 'All right?' knew then he had been telling her that soon there would be no turning back, she'd had her chance then, and what had she done but agreed, 'All right' in return.

Impatiently Tully tried to get away from her thoughts, but there was no escaping them. Where Yate was sleeping tonight she had no idea, but it was a certainty he had no intention of resting his head on the pillow next to hers. Tears came then, she knew they were tears of her tattered emotions, but could do nothing to stop them. If only Richard hadn't taken that money she would be with Howard ... Howard, oh God, what had come over her? She loved Howard—she knew she did. It didn't help in her tussle for sleep that thoughts of Howard should join those of Yate. Howard had never made her feel the way Yate had.

How long she lay there wrestling with her inner soul she had no idea—it had seemed like hours before her tears had dried and exhaustion of mind and spirit took her off in the arms of Morpheus. Marian bringing her an early cup of tea on Sunday morning brought her up from a heavy sleep.

She remembered instantly everything that had gone on the night before and wished with all her heart that Marian had left her to sleep until it was time to go back to London.

'Good morning, Marian,' she said, struggling to sit up and smile at the young maid.

'Good morning, Miss Vickery,' Marian answered shyly as she put the tray down. 'Er—can I run your bath or anything? Mrs Everley said I was to help you all I could.'

'That was kind of Mrs Everley,' Tully smiled, declining her offer. 'But I expect she could do with your help this morning.'

'Oh, that's all right, Mrs Everley doesn't have to do much, there's plenty of help—Mrs Everley only supervises now, Mrs Meachem won't let her do any of the hard work.'

This was quite a long speech coming from the shy Marian, and Tully thought perhaps she might keep her talking a while longer, hoping to keep her mind from going over the same tangled thoughts that had kept her awake last night. But the breakthrough into Marian's shyness didn't last, and the young girl said if there was nothing she could do to help her she would be off.

It wasn't as early as she had thought, Tully saw when she glanced at the watch Yate had loaned her. To try and go back to sleep was not only impossible, but bad-mannered into the bargain. She guessed since it was now nine o'clock, that everyone else would be downstairs having breakfast, and although she wasn't hungry, the more urgent thought of what would she do if Yate, his breakfast finished, decided to come looking for her, made her instantly alert.

In a flash she was out of bed, the bath taps gushing water. Fifteen minutes later she was dressed in a cotton dress of a warm pink colour, and was sitting before the dressing table mirror wondering what if anything she could do to disguise the fact that her eyes looked tired from her shortened night.

Going downstairs took a great deal of courage. To enter

the breakfast room called for much more. Her hand on the door handle, Tully thought her limbs were going to refuse to advance any further, but telling herself she had more backbone than to wilt should, as she expected, Yate be there, she lifted her head proudly and opened the door.

CHAPTER SEVEN

YATE *was* there. He was the first person she saw seated at the table as she entered the room. Her swift glance left him as he politely got to his feet, and she saw Jackie and Bart were there too, though there was no sign of Mrs Meachem.

'Good morning,' she offered generally, and when the answering greetings were over she heard Yate say:

'Come and sit here, Tully. What would you like to eat? There's ...'

'Just toast, please, if I may.'

How normal and everyday it all sounded! But it wasn't normal and everyday, she was feeling sick inside, and after that first quick glance at Yate, seeing him looking as large as ever in his fawn slacks and lightweight sweater, she hadn't dared to look at him again.

'Marmalade?'

Tully turned to Jackie who was passing the marmalade over to her. 'Thank you,' she said, and felt an uncomfortable silence come over the table as no one seemed to have anything else to say. 'I'm sorry I'm late,' she apologised, seeing everyone else was at the toast stage and trying to inject some normality into the atmosphere.

'We'll forgive you,' said Bart, and she sent him a smile. 'We've been up ages. Marian was going to bring your tea up about eight, but I heard Yate telling her to leave you for another hour.'

Tully thought it was expected of her to look at Yate and thank him for his consideration, but regardless of whatever anyone else expected, it was beyond her to do so.

'We all had a late night,' she heard Yate chip in, almost as if he was trying to help her, she thought, then discounted that he would want to help her with anything. 'Mother isn't up yet, so you're not the last,' he was saying when she felt Bart's eyes on her.

She looked across at Bart, saw from his expression that he had seen her eyes were looking tired, and suddenly the air was electric as he said, '*You* look as though you had a *later night* than any of us.' She went scarlet and felt Yate's tense movement beside her. Bart's remark could have been perfectly innocent, but she hadn't thought so, and she guessed neither had Yate.

'For your information, Bart,' he said, and there was ice in his voice that made her teeth jump, 'Tully is not sleeping with me. Your remark was not only ungallant but the innuendo unjustified—I think you owe Tully an apology.'

'My God, you've changed,' Bart snapped back. 'It's not like you to have access to a female and not follow up your advantage.'

Tully looked down at the tablecloth, then as if impelled her eyes sought Yate. His face was white with temper, she saw, and for one horrifying moment she thought he was going to yank his brother out of his wheelchair and throw him across the room. She saw his hands clench hard as he fought for control.

'Tully is occupying the apartment in the west wing,' he enlightened his brother. 'I am sleeping in one of the rooms opposite. I'm waiting, Bart.'

Tully had to but in, anything to cool down this moment when both brothers seemed set to have a go at each other. 'Please,' she said, 'don't ...' She broke off, there was no need to say any more. Bart turned his eyes on her and saw the embarrassed colour staining her cheeks, and his temper seemed to leave him.

'I'm sorry, Tully,' he said, and she could see he was sincere. 'Brother Yate was right to pull me up,' he smiled winningly at her. 'I suppose I should have known it would all be very different when he fell in love.' Bart had got it all so wrong, but the last thing she was going to do was put him right since it appeared that the vessel of antagonism was now sailing in calmer waters. 'Yate would cherish the woman he loves,' Bart added quietly, 'and though wanting her near to him, he would do nothing to shame her.'

To look at Yate now that Bart's apology had been voiced would have taken far more courage than she could own to. From the sound of it, Bart knew his brother very well—even if he had got it all wrong in thinking that Yate loved her. Yet he made it sound as though the girl with whom Yate did fall in love would be a very lucky girl indeed.

She was grateful to Jackie for introducing the Boat Race as a topic of conversation. And as breakfast continued with tempers now well under control, Tully couldn't but wonder how Bart had arrived at the conclusion that Yate was in love with her. That was until it came to her that hadn't that been the impression Yate had been trying to give ever since they had got here? When she had taxed him with shadowing her last night for fear she might become light-fingered, he'd said then that she had got it all wrong. That 'darling' he had dropped out loud enough for Bart to hear last night too, she had known then that it hadn't been for her benefit, he'd changed soon enough when no one else was about. Suddenly she was certain of it. Yate Meachem wanted his family to think he was in love with her. Now why would he want to do that? He hadn't been home for nearly a year, Mrs Everley had let that drop ...

'More coffee, Tully?'

'Er——' She became aware that everyone was looking at her. 'Er—no, thanks, Jackie—I think I've had enough.'

Bart preferred to be independent in his wheelchair, so with Jackie by him, as soon as breakfast was finished he wheeled himself out of the room. Yate was already standing and Tully wondered what she did now. She didn't want to be alone with him, but for a different set of reasons from the ones she had nursed yesterday.

'Come for a walk, Tully.'

He wasn't asking, it was a statement, and without the idea she had that he seemed to want to give the impression he was in love with her, she realised that Yate wasn't likely to want her to be where he couldn't see her anyway. No, in his eyes she had criminal tendencies and it was a case of wherever I go, you go.

'All right,' she said, knowing she could say no other, and blushed furiously as those two words brought between them memories she was trying to forget.

'Go and get a cardigan or something,' Yate instructed her, and if he had seen her blush she was thankful to her heart that he saw better than to comment on it.

They took a path to the right of the Grange, a silence between them unbroken. Yate seemed to have something on his mind, and was in no mood for conversation. Tully would like to have asked him why he had defended her virtue so vigorously this morning against Bart's barely veiled slighting comment, but could never ask, she realised, as the frightening thought came that if she did so some mention, if only briefly, might be made of last night after she had stubbed her toe. That episode had to be buried with all speed.

They had been walking for some time when they came to stand by a five-barred gate. Tully stood silently by as Yate rested his arms on the top spar and looked out into the distance.

'Has Bart been in a wheelchair long?' she asked, wanting to know the answer, but more than that finding Yate's ignoring her as though she wasn't there getting through to her.

'About a year,' he said matter-of-factly, offering no other information.

'What happened?' It was a natural question, she thought, but as Yate turned his head and gave her a hard-eyed look, she had the feeling she was trespassing on something he had no wish to talk about.

'Car accident,' he said briefly, and then she thought she understood.

About a year, he had said—it was about a year since Yate had been home. He must have been driving the car and having come out of the accident unscathed he couldn't bear to talk about it. Strange—she remembered thinking on the way down what a good driver he was. Perhaps he hadn't always been, perhaps it had taken that crash to make him more aware of what was going on around him. She was beginning to understand a lot of other things too that had puzzled her. This must be the cause of the animosity between the two brothers. That smile when Bart had seen Yate laugh meant that the affection Bart had for his brother was still there beneath the surface, but his bitterness that in driving the car Yate had robbed him of the use of his legs had overshadowed that love.

'I'm sorry,' she said quietly, and watched while Yate took his arms away from the gate and turned his full attention on her.

'Why should you be sorry?'

So it still hurt? Sure now she was right in her surmisings, she said gently, 'You were driving, weren't you?' and heard the awful sound of his mirthless laugh.

'You have it all wrong, Miss Vickery—Bart was alone in that car when he crashed it.'

'Oh.'

'Do you want another stab at it?' he asked cruelly, 'or are you ready to go back?'

Without speaking, conscious that his cruel sarcasm had cut her very deep, she turned to face the way they had come and set off. But she hadn't gone far before she felt a hand on her shoulder spinning her round and she was facing a furious-looking Yate. She had no idea just then who his fury was directed at—himself, her or Bart.

'Don't go running away—you're dying of curiosity, aren't you? Surely if you've got enough nerve to enter my business premises in the dark of night, you have enough nerve to stay and ask the questions that are ferreting around in your mind?'

It was almost as though he now wanted her to know, she thought. As though he had carried the weight of guilt around for too long and now wanted to be free of it. For she was sure all at once, as sure as she was breathing, if somewhat erratically, that he was guilty of something. Then as suddenly, she was as certain she didn't want to know, felt for some unknown reason his weight of guilt would be too heavy for her shoulders, and she tried to turn out of his grip, to turn and run away from him.

'Oh no, you don't! You stirred up this whole thing. Wouldn't you say it's only decent to stay and hear the rest of it?'

'You're just dying to unload some of your guilt, aren't you?' Her head came up, stung that to get her reaction he hadn't been able to resist flinging her past misdemeanours in her face. 'Go on, then, Mr Way-above-sin Meachem, tell me what it is that's eating your heart out. It's obvious that you had something to do with Bart's crash. What was it? Was it your car he was driving when he crashed? Was the braking system faulty? Was the steering mechanism all to pot?'

'None of those things, my dear Sherlock,' Yate said grimly. 'Bart was driving his own car.' Then as though he was reliving it, his face seemed to grow pale as she watched. 'Bart was upset. He raced out of the house—there was a roar as he took off—pointless to go after him he'd only put his foot down and maybe kill himself. The next thing we knew the police were at the house saying there'd been an accident—and that *bitch* Rowena was having hysterics.'

Yate had let go his hold on her, but Tully didn't move, couldn't move. There was a look of such pain, such anguish on his face, she couldn't have moved then if her life depended upon it. Who was Rowena? It was a name she hadn't heard mentioned this weekend—though the answer to that wasn't important just then. Yate had gone far away deep in some black anguish of his own—it seemed vital to get him back from the ache of his thoughts.

'You said Bart was upset,' she said softly. 'Why was he upset, Yate?'

At the sound of her voice Yate seemed to realize with surprise that she was still standing there. 'What?' he asked, and she knew then that he hadn't heard her question.

'I asked what had happened to make Bart upset,' she repeated, and didn't want to know at all as she saw a terrible cynical look come over his face. But before she could retract her question, he was saying harshly:

'Bart was engaged to Rowena at the time. He wandered from his bedroom one night and found her in bed with me.'

Tully felt the breath go out of her as his hard unvarnished words hit her ears, no regret showing, no remorse, just a plain statement of fact, and as her eyes widened in painful disbelief Yate turned away from her.

'Curiosity satisfied?' he asked.

Tully didn't wait for any more, she took to her heels and ran. She had to run faster and faster to get away from the thoughts that chased her. Breathless and panting, with a stitch in her side, she reached the house. Jackie was just going into the drawing room as she sped along the hall, but Tully barely saw her as she raced past her and up the stairs of the west wing.

Had she been a man she could never have treated her brother so, she thought wildly as lack of further energy caused her to collapse into a chair once she had gained the sitting room of the apartment. Her love for her brother would have her doing anything to save him from pain and she just couldn't comprehend how Yate could have done what he had told her with his own lips he had done.

No wonder there was antagonism just beneath the surface between the two of them! That Yate could have made this Rowena his mistress knowing that Bart must love her, was incomprehensible. It was sick, that's what it was, sick. No wonder Yate hadn't shown his face in nearly twelve months—yet his mother, and Mrs Everley, they'd been overjoyed on seeing him there. Didn't they know what had gone on to cause Bart to have his accident? To drive off in his car, probably not knowing what he was doing or where he was going? And why, she paused to wonder, had Yate come home at all?—And why bring her?

It didn't take very many minutes for her to come up with what she thought must be the right answer, particularly as she recalled the way Yate hadn't denied it when Bart had suggested his brother was in love with her. She saw it all then. Yate had wanted to come home, might even have wanted to mend things between him and Bart. Bart's engagement to Jackie had meant that Bart was no longer hung up over Rowena, but just in case Bart might think that the same thing might happen, that he might come in and find Yate in bed with his new fiancée Jackie, Yate had obviated any speculation in that area by bringing his own girl-friend along, and seeming to anyone who cared to watch as though he was hard put to it to let her out of his sight. She couldn't quite figure out why then had Yate so vehemently defended her at Bart's obvious conclusion that she and Yate were bed-mates, but she thought she had enough to go on with, without complicating the issue by looking for the answer to that one.

Unable to sit still, Tully got up and went into the bedroom, pausing by the dressing table where she tried to pinch some colour into her pale cheeks. She was vaguely aware of having ignored Jackie in the hall downstairs, and as this certainty grew she realised she had better go down and apologise to her. She'd better go now, she didn't want to leave it until Yate came back, didn't want him to know she had been so upset she had rushed past Jackie, seeing her, yet not seeing her.

She tried the drawing room first thinking that had been the room she had seen Jackie entering, and luck was with her as she found Jackie alone. Jackie looked up from the crossword she was doing and the smile of welcome on her face told Tully she was not permanently offended.

'I owe you an apology, Jackie,' she said without hesitation. 'I was a bit—er—out of sorts when I came in—I'm afraid I . . .'

'That's all right,' Jackie said kindly. 'I could see from your face you were all hot and bothered.' She broke off, having already decided what had been the matter after having seen Tully go out with Yate and come haring back on her own. 'I always feel just like that when Bart and I have a few words—though thank goodness it doesn't happen often. You'll be fine when you see Yate again,' she assured her.

Tully knew Jackie meant well, and liking the girl felt she would have liked to have confided in her, but knew she couldn't. For a start she didn't know how much, if anything, Jackie knew of Rowena, and in the face of Jackie's happiness she definitely wasn't going to say anything that might put a frown on the other girl's serene forehead.

'I expect I shall,' she agreed, ready to leave the subject right there. 'Where's Bart?' she asked, knowing he couldn't be very far away.

'He's gone to his room to do his exercises.' Jackie sighed, and Tully knew the sigh was on Bart's behalf, not Jackie's, when the girl said, 'Physically he's in tip-top shape—the doctors have said he should be walking by now, that's why he agreed for us to become engaged. But though he's fanatical about doing his exercises, nothing seems to be happening.'

This was something Yate had not told her, yet he must know. She was learning enough about him to believe that he would have a hot line somewhere to someone in the know and be kept up to date with any progress his brother was making. So Bart wasn't doomed to a wheelchair for the rest of his life? She couldn't help but feel glad as that thought penetrated, and absurdly, it came to her that she was as glad for Yate's sake as for Bart's. She dashed the thought away from her as Jackie said:

'Bart has come on wonderfully since we met.' She smiled reminiscently, 'He was like a bear with a sore head when I first met him.' He had one thing in common with his brother, then. 'We met in a car park,' Jackie told her, and seeing Tully was interested went on, 'There was just one space and our two cars—I still swear I was first there. Anyway, we had quite a slanging match from our car windows, then I ignored him and grabbed the space. Then from my rear window I saw another car pull out, which left a space for Bart. I was messing about, still furious, getting my library books and odds and ends together, then when I looked in my mirror again I saw Bart setting up his wheelchair before he heaved himself out. I nearly died of shame. I felt such a meanie I dropped my books when I got out of my car. After I'd picked them up I just knew I would have to go over and apologise. But when I got up to him,' she recalled, 'he just sat glowering at me, independence written all over him—I still don't know what came over me, but instead of saying sorry, I said, "See, if you'd waited just ten seconds there wouldn't have been any need to lose your filthy temper." Honestly, Tully, I thought he was going to leap from his chair and land me one, then suddenly he laughed.' Jackie smiled to herself as she remembered, then went on, 'And then, when I could see he was as independent as Harry, he said, "I'm going to the library too—you can give me a push." ʼ

Tully's romantic heart was touched by Jackie's story, but as she looked at the other girl she saw her lively face cloud over. 'I love him so much, Tully, but I know he won't agree for us to marry until he can stand on his own two feet for the ceremony. Bart seems to have something blocking the way of him getting back the use of his legs,' she confided. 'We thought deciding to get engaged would do the trick, but that hasn't worked. Then Mrs Meachem thought seeing Yate down here again might be the answer— I don't know if you know, but Bart and Yate had an awful row about a year ago and hadn't spoken to each other since.'

Tully thought then that Jackie did know about Rowena and warmed to the girl that out of thought for her as Yate's girl-friend, this time it was Jackie who was keeping silent about Rowena.

'Anyway,' Jackie continued, 'Mrs Meachem said that Yate sat with Bart day and night while Bart lay unconscious in the hospital—Bart was delicate as a child, apparently—if the wind changed direction he would get a cold, and since their father died when they were very young, Yate's always felt protective towards his brother. Anyway,' Jackie said again, 'when Bart's mother told me all this I agreed it was worth a try, so Mrs Meachem telephoned Yate and asked him to come home and help celebrate Bart's engagement, she told him it might help to get Bart walking again, and he told her he would think about it but that he couldn't see that if the love of a good woman couldn't perform the miracle how the hell we thought Bart seeing *him* was going to do it.'

'That sounds exactly like Yate,' Tully opined, actually seeing him in her mind's eye saying the words. She and Jackie exchanged wry grins.

'You can imagine how excited Mrs Meachem and I

were when Yate rang before we'd even had breakfast yesterday to say not only would he be here, but that he was bringing someone rather special with him.'

So he had decided his plan of action even then, Tully thought, no longer feeling like grinning. Then the drawing room door opened and she knew her tête-à-tête with Jackie was over when the door stayed open as Mrs Meachem came in and with a not too polite swear word as his chair hit the woodwork Bart wheeled himself in behind her.

'Where's Yate?' Mrs Meachem asked Tully lightly as she came and sat herself down on the settee beside her. Tully was glad of Jackie answering for her.

'I've just seen him go by the window,' Jackie said. Then turning to Bart, 'How did it go?'

'Could do with a drink,' he answered, but there was a special smile in his eyes for Jackie as he looked at her, Tully noticed.

Why she fully expected Yate to join them in the drawing room Tully didn't know, for she already suspected that Yate rarely did what was expected of him. But hearing his footsteps coming along the hall, she had her face all set to break into a smile should any of the others happen to glance her way. The footsteps didn't falter as they reached the drawing room door, but went firmly on.

Was he still in that foul mood? Tully wondered, and feeling uncomfortable suddenly that everyone would expect Yate to come looking for her, or so she thought, she realised there was only one way of finding out. Mrs Meachem had just finished saying that lunch should be ready in half an hour, and Bart was asking if anyone would care for a glass of sherry, when Tully got to her feet.

'Not for me, Bart, thanks, I'll just go and see where Yate has got to.'

To anyone interested, she mused as she headed for the west wing, it would look as though she couldn't bear to have Yate out of her sight for a minute. If they only knew!

But dislike him as she did, and though unable to find anything worthy in his goings on with Rowena, now that she
was aware of his reasons for blackmailing her into coming
with him this weekend, she wanted to help too. She wasn't
sure what she could do to help, but if she could do anything
that might go towards releasing the mental block that was
holding Bart's use of his legs, then she would co-operate
fully. She and Yate would be leaving in a few hours, so she
didn't know what help she could be, but all Yate's talk of
wanting her for his mistress this weekend, she saw, had
been one gigantic bluff. She was positive now that Yate's
only interest was that Bart should walk again, sure that un-
derneath the hostility there was a deep affection between
the two, as deep as hers for Richard.

She thought Yate might be in the sitting room of the
small apartment, but he wasn't there. Silently Tully with-
drew and closed the door before turning round. There were
several doors along the landing for her to choose from, but
at her knock at the one directly opposite the sitting room,
she thought she heard a movement from within. Without
waiting for an answer—he'd probably tell her to go away
if his mood hadn't changed—she opened the door.

Yate had been in the act of changing and his hands stilled
momentarily from buttoning his shirt as he saw her.

'Do come in,' he bade her sarcastically.

'I ... I did knock,' she answered, feeling suddenly nervous of the glint in his eyes.

'I heard you. However, since you were so eager to see me
you couldn't wait until I'd finished dressing and came to
let you in—Come here. I'm always willing to oblige a lady.'

'I'm sure you are,' Tully said on a spurt of temper. 'It
doesn't matter if that lady is already spoken for either, does
it?'

Immediately the words were out she regretted them.
She saw the look of instant fury that passed over his features
before he turned his back on her to reach for his tie.

'What a sweet old-fashioned way of putting it,' he said sardonically. 'But then you are old-fashioned, aren't you, Tully?—in some things.'

She knew then she had done nothing to sweeten his black mood, and knew she would have to apologise if she was going to be able to talk to him, even though 'in some things' was an unwanted reference to the thief he thought she was.

'I'm sorry, Yate—I shouldn't have said that.' He ignored her and went on tying his tie. 'Look, Yate, I—I know you don't like me—at the moment I don't think you're liking yourself very much either.' She couldn't think why she had said that other than it had just come to her that it was true. But she saw she had his attention now. His tie correctly in place, he was ignoring her no longer. 'Jackie has just been telling me about Bart—about the very good chance there is that he'll walk again.' She wished Yate would say something instead of pinning her with that dark look—he didn't even look as if he was wondering what she was leading up to. But she couldn't wish she had never started, she was sincere in wanting to help.

'Jackie intimated that Bart has some sort of psychological block preventing him from walking,' she began again, remembering Yate had once called her an amateur psychologist. 'It—well, it occurred to me that it might have something to do with the fact that Bart might not feel secure with Jackie with you around . . .' Oh dear, he was giving her one of those looks that terrified her. Her voice died in her throat; any minute now he would be opening that door and throwing her down the stairs.

'Do continue,' he said, his voice harsh with control. 'Don't imagine I have any sensitive feelings at anything you're saying.' His sarcasm was biting, but Tully lifted her head a degree or two higher. They had never pussyfooted around—plain speaking was about the only honesty between them.

'Very well,' she said, a haughty expression covering her

own sensitivity. 'What I came up here to say is this. I've realised exactly why you wanted me to come here with you. It had nothing to do with your needing a m-mistress,' she wished she hadn't faltered over that word, 'other than in name only.' She stopped, beginning to grow confused as she tacked that bit on. Yate had been forceful this morning in denying he had slept with her, and she hadn't yet reasoned why he should do that if ... 'What I'm trying to say, Yate,' she went on, knowing that by now he would think she was babbling, 'is that if you think it might help Bart to believe that you and I—that-that we're in l-love, then I'm—willing.'

She couldn't look him in the face as she came to the end of what she had to say. She had been sure she was right, had been sure Yate had seen the situation the same way, but in the silence that followed her words, she was beginning to think she had got it all wrong. Maybe Yate didn't care for his brother after all. Maybe ...

'So you've reasoned it out that I didn't intend to have you for my mistress this weekend, have you?' His voice was less harsh, giving her the courage to look at him again. His face was still stern, but there was something in his eyes that was thawing out the ice, then it was all spoilt as he asked coolly, 'What did you think that little exercise last night was all about? I was ready to take you, Tully.'

Her face flamed. This sort of plain speaking was hard to take. 'B-but you didn't, did you?' she said chokily, and wished with all her heart that she could have added, 'because I stopped you.' A fresh wave of colour threatened to drown her.

'No, I didn't,' he agreed, and she was glad he didn't add that he could have done. He knew as well as she that there had been no opposition. But he did add, and there was a strangely gentle note in his voice. 'Poor little Tully—you're completely out of your depth, aren't you? You were last night—I should have realised that without having to ask after your innocence.' And at that word innocence he must have remembered as she did, she thought, that she was far from innocent in the matter of trying to rob him. The gentle note had gone when next he spoke.

'I don't get you at all,' he said grimly. 'You must have worked out for yourself by now that I no longer have any hold over you,' and in case he hadn't elucidated the point. 'I can hardly take criminal proceedings against you for it to come out in court that after said crime I took you to meet my family and their friends, and that you spent a night in my home as a guest. So why, when you're free to slam the door shut on the lot of us, are you willing to further this charade by pretending to be in love with someone you hate?'

Did she hate him? Tully wasn't sure any more. She had felt no hate towards him when she had been in his arms last night. Hastily she turned her mind away from such thoughts. 'Your family have been kind to me,' she said. 'I may hate you, Yate, but I like your mother, Jackie and Bart. In a few hours I shall be away from here. It seems a very small thing to do to repay their kindness, if it will help Bart.'

'Ah yes, Bart,' drawled Yate. They had diverted somewhat from the point of discussion. 'You were accurate in your surmise that I was trying to give the impression that cupid's dart had hit me,' he said slowly. 'Perhaps a little co-operation from you in that direction wouldn't come amiss. Anything is worth trying if it will get Bart on his pins again. I'll confess,' he said, and she knew she was in for some plain speaking, 'that I wasn't feeling very friendly towards you when I came in—it could well have showed through when we all sat down together at lunch time. So —thank you, Tully, for bearding the lions' den, though I never did doubt your courage.'

And while Tully was still wondering if, in a roundabout way, she had just received a compliment, he moved until he was standing very close to her, then lowered his head and gently kissed her.

'Come on,' he said, breaking the kiss abruptly. 'I'm starving, and you must be too.'

Yate had his arm about her waist as he ushered her into the drawing room. And knowing it was she who had suggested she co-operate with him in this role of mutual love, Tully realised with alarm that had to be quietened that she found his arm at the back of her in no way distasteful.

CHAPTER EIGHT

FOR the first time when in a room with Yate and Bart, Tully's overcharged senses picked up that the tension between the brothers was missing. Not that either of them had much to say to each other as the midday meal progressed, but their silences were not strained. She wondered if anyone else had noticed it, certainly Yate's mother seemed more relaxed than she had done. This weekend must have been a strain on her too, she realised then, and Tully's smile was open and warm as she looked at Mrs Meachem as she refused her hostess's offer of more vegetables.

'I've hardly seen you to get to know you, Tully,' Mrs Meachem said, passing the sprout dish over to Bart. 'There was no time with everyone here last night, and I just can't rush first thing. Bart takes after me—he's a real sleepyhead first thing in the morning.'

'I did make it to the breakfast table this morning,' Bart put in teasingly.

'By the skin of your teeth, I'll bet,' his mother came back.

Bart looked at Tully, and she knew an uncomfortable moment when she expected him to refer to breakfast being almost over before she had appeared. She saw Bart's look transfer from her to Yate—watched worriedly while the two brothers looked levelly at each other. She hadn't forgotten the way Yate had gone for Bart in her defence that morning and she dreaded more of the same happening. Then suddenly, like sun coming out after rain, Bart grinned at Yate, a sort of 'I want to be friends, big brother' type of grin. 'You're right,' Bart told his mother, 'I made it by the

127

skin of my teeth.' And then while Tully watched, Yate's mouth quirked and he was grinning back at Bart.

The happiness Tully experienced at the unspoken exchange between the two was out of all proportion she felt. Her eyes went again to Yate and she saw he was watching her. Then suddenly there was sunshine in her direction, for while Yate, unsmiling now, continued to look at her, his lips suddenly parted and she was on the receiving end of his completely unsuspicious grin. Her heart turned over and she was totally unaware that she was grinning foolishly back until Bart said:

'Hey—break it up, you two!'

Tully looked down at her plate feeling her cheeks growing pink, heard Bart say, 'Methinks my brother doth protest too much,' and was in a fog to know what he meant until she recalled Bart's remark about wedding march talk when Yate had called her 'darling' last night. Yate had said then that it had been a slip of the tongue, no more.

Mrs Meachem seemed to be sharing the same fog as she had felt, Tully saw, but all she said was, 'Don't you two start talking in riddles.' But from the way she said it, Tully guessed that Yate and his brother must often have confused her with their talk in the old days. Was everything going to come right between them at last? She was forced to abandon any more thoughts she might have on the subject as Mrs Meachem decided to ignore her two sons and addressed one or two remarks to Jackie before turning her attention to Tully.

'Yate was telling me you lived in London, Tully, have you lived there long?'

'About two years.' That statement sounded a bit flat, so Tully mentioned the area she lived in, adding that she and her brother shared an apartment.

'Oh good, I'm glad you're not on your own. Do you have any other family?'

Tully knew Mrs Meachem was just being kind in getting her to speak about herself, but aware Yate was listening would much rather she hadn't asked.

'Not now,' she had to own. 'My mother died four years ago, my stepfather two years later. Richard thought we would stand a better chance of finding jobs if we moved to London—we were living in a small village at the time,' she explained.

'You weren't working before you went to London?' Tully knew Mrs Meachem wasn't prying, but showing a natural interest in the girl her son had brought to the house, and she couldn't not answer her.

'No,' she confessed. 'I'd never worked at a job before I went to London.' She heard Yate offering to fill Jackie's wine glass and thought he had lost interest in the conversation she was having with his mother, so she was more natural than she would otherwise have been. 'We had a fairly large house—though not as large as this,' she hastened to add with a smile. 'My mother and stepfather enjoyed life, I'm glad to say,' her eyes took on a loving light as she thought of them. 'They were often away for weeks at a time, so I more or less took over the running of the house.' There had been no more or less about it—they'd had ample staff to help, and she had enjoyed what she had done.

'And you decided to give up the house after your step-father died,' Mrs Meachem said understandingly. 'You thought you'd like to try your hand at something different?'

There had been very little choice, but Tully nodded. She didn't want to tell an outright lie, but didn't want to say that since she hadn't been trained for anything she would have snatched the hand of the first employer who offered her work. Yate didn't appear to be listening, but one never knew with him, and she was still wary of letting something slip that might make things awkward for Richard, though what she wasn't sure. But she was overwhelmingly conscious that Richard still worked for the Meachem Organisation and that Yate didn't put any credence on her brother's non-involvement with that money.

'I've always had a flair for languages,' she said, aware Mrs Meachem was waiting to hear more. 'It's lovely to be able to use them.'

She was grateful when the conversation became more general. Then Yate was saying he had some paper work to do later that night and that they would be leaving for London about four. So not too long after lunch Tully went upstairs to pack her things together. She met Marian on the way and the young girl offered to do her packing for her, but Tully refused her offer, saying she had plenty of time.

All in all, she thought, as she folded her clothes, most of them unworn this weekend, she was glad the moment to leave was almost here. True, the weekend had turned out to be vastly different from what she had been expecting, thank goodnss, but it was no thanks to her that she hadn't shared that bed with Yate last night. Hurriedly she turned her head away from the bed. What had come over her? She couldn't put it down to too much champagne, much as she would like to have done. She had always had an inward conviction that drunk or sober it was impossible for one to act outside one's true self, and she had certainly been far from drunk.

She heard a sound in the sitting room through the open door, and wasn't too surprised when Yate walked through, his eyes going to the suitcase she had all but finished packing.

'Marian could have done that for you,' he said, coming further into the room.

'She did offer, but I told her I could do it.'

'You're used to having a maid pack for you, though,' he said, and she knew then he had missed none of what she had told his mother at lunch time.

'Well, yes—sometimes.' She didn't want him here. Didn't know what point he had come to make—if any point at all. Yate Meachem would do exactly what he thought he would and to hell with who got hurt; she had to look no further than Bart and his ex-fiancée Rowena to know that was true. 'Are you ready to go?' she asked, beginning to grow confused just by seeing him standing there idly eyeing her frilly underwear which just happened to be on the top of her case. With more haste than was necessary she placed the dress she had worn last night on top, covering her flimsy garments from his glance. She saw the beginnings of a smile start to curve his lips upwards and looked away. Damn him, he knew he had her confused.

'Are you going to tell your brother you've been away with me?' he asked suddenly.

Tully hadn't any idea what she was going to tell Richard. 'I don't know,' she confessed honestly. Richard would go straight into panic if she told him she had been caught putting that money back. 'I shall have to tell him something—but I think, since he works for you,' she tacked on hastily, 'that I would rather he didn't know where I've been.'

'Hmm——' That alone told her he still wasn't prepared to believe Richard's hand wasn't in the attempted burglary somewhere. 'You needn't come back with me if you don't want to,' Yate said after a moment.

'Not come back with you?' What was he hinting? That he was fed up with seeing her? That he wanted her to find her own way back to London? Her lips clamped together until it came to her that Yate wouldn't hint at a thing like that—he would tell her outright.

'It occurred to me that since your brother thinks you're on holiday with the boy-friend, you might have some trouble with your explanations—You can stay on here for the rest of the week if it will help you.'

Yate Meachem was actually offering to help her! It was an idea, though, and sorely tempting since he himself wouldn't be there. But ...

'No, thanks—I'll think of something to tell Richard. Besides,' she said trying a little sarcasm of her own, 'you would never rest in your bed knowing I was loose among your family silver.'

'Your consideration for my sleepless nights does you credit, Tallulah.' Her sarcasm was a poor thing compared to his, she realised. 'From the look of your tired eyes this morning I think your concern is misplaced.' Her cheeks flamed as she knew he had known they would. 'Had I thought my leaving you to your chaste little self would have made you cry,' so he knew about that too—did nothing escape him!—'I should have stayed and you really would have had something to cry about this morning.'

What could she answer to that? He knew full well how mixed up she was feeling, loving Howard the way she did yet having wanted another man to make love to her. If she thought it would do any good she would tell him she didn't want to talk about it, but she knew that wouldn't stop him.

'Well, you didn't stay, did you?' she challenged, and as he made as if to step towards her. 'And I'm glad you didn't,' she said hastily, thinking he might have read she wanted him to take up from where he had left off from the challenging way her words had come out. 'Please don't come near me, Yate—y-you know—that is——' She took a deep breath then tried again. 'Look—you know much more about women than I'll ever know about men.' He must do, she reasoned, to know she had cried after he had gone. 'I don't know what came over me last night—I ... I'm in love with Howard.' She flicked a glance at him, saw that his lips had tightened at Howard's name. He probably thought her love for Howard was an insignificant thing if she could respond to him so readily, she thought, and knew she stood to become more confused than ever if she followed that line of thought through.

'I'm in love with Howard,' she stated more firmly. 'That I—acted the way I did last night must have been because—because I—er—somehow—er—needed to have Howard with me, and . . . and . . .' her voice tapered off as she saw the stormy expression that came over Yate's face.

'So you thought you would use me as a substitute lover,' he snarled with an anger that was suddenly white-hot. And then he moved—moved so rapidly, Tully didn't even have the chance to back away. She felt the iron bands of his arms around her, heard his voice grating, 'Well, imagine this is your tepid lover,' and before she could stop him he had taken brutal possession of her mouth.

He was giving no pleasure in that kiss; it was an act of pure violation. His hands moved angrily over her, pulling her roughly against him, moulding her every curve to him, his lips bruising hers, giving her no chance to reject him or respond, just taking, taking, taking. Then as suddenly, she was free, pushed away from him as though he felt tainted at having touched her.

His eyes flaming, that blue inferno scorched into her ashen face. Then as if he couldn't bear to be in the same room with her, his arm snaked out to lift her case. 'Be downstairs in five minutes,' he ordered, then strode out.

Tully took four of those minutes to sit down trying to calm herself. What had that been all about? How had they got on to the subject of last night anyway? They had been discussing the possibility of her staying on at the Grange in order to avoid giving Richard a difficult explanation. Nothing made any sense any more. She was getting all tied up with why Yate Meachem should have made the offer at all when from his point of view he must have the gravest doubts about her honesty. That coupled with that unloving, as though he hated her, assault on her just now was a direct contrast to the kindness of his offer.

She looked at the watch on her wrist—she'd better get a move on. It was five past four now, she didn't want him to come back looking for her—her complete freedom from him was little over an hour away.

'Ah, there you are,' said Yate when she entered the drawing room where his mother, Jackie and Bart were assembled.

Tully had thought it unlikely from the hate in his kiss that he would bother to speak to her again. But of course, Bart was here and she remembered it had been she who had approached Yate suggesting she had no objection to pretending she was in love with him.

'Have I kept you waiting?' She forced a warm smile in his direction though she wouldn't meet his eyes, and was saved having to say anything further to him in the general farewells that followed.

Yate's mother had the same tears in her eyes, she noticed, as Mrs Meachem said goodbye to Yate that had been there when she had greeted him. She understood now why it had meant so much to her that he had come home. Mrs Meachem had a special goodbye to say to her too.

'Thank you for coming with Yate, Tully, we shall be pleased to see you at any time.'

Tully sat in the car beside Yate as they drove off, aware that Mrs Meachem, as well as Bart, thought the feelings between her and her elder son were vastly different from what they were.

All pretence of being a couple in love fell completely away as the car sped nearer and nearer to London. Not that she had expected anything other—she didn't want it any other way, for goodness' sake. She had been paying the price for her misdeeds, as soon as Yate dropped her outside her apartment, that account would be settled.

Yate drove efficiently and well. His silence could have been taken for concentration, but she knew it wasn't. They had nothing to say to each other and Yate was above making pleasantries he didn't feel. Well that was all right with her too. There was only one word she wanted to say to him, and that was goodbye.

They were about ten minutes away from her apartment when Yate said, 'You've been a tremendous help this weekend—thank you.'

She hadn't expected his thanks. The way she saw it, she couldn't have done any other. 'That's all right,' she said, her voice sounding as cool as his.

'Knowing how you feel about me, it was very thoughtful of you to suggest you act as though you were in love with me.'

She hadn't thought she had done much in that line either. That grin they had shared, which Bart had seen, had been spontaneous with nothing of an act about it, though perhaps she had sent him warmer glances than she might otherwise have done, when he had held back her chair for her, when he had touched her shoulder as she had left the room.

'You could have acted that way at lunch time without mentioning it to me,' he said.

She had thought about it, he needn't worry. 'What, and have you choke on your soup?' she said dryly. 'It had crossed by mind,' she went on, 'but since you already think so badly of me—I wasn't ready to risk your getting the idea I was playing up to you for what I could get out of you.'

'You want nothing from me?'

What sort of a question was that? Had he forgotten he was under the impression she had tried to rob his safe? Was he perhaps remembering the way she had welcomed his kisses last night? Did he think she was expecting some sort of payment for doing what she had in the first place been forced to do? She felt the blood begin to rush through her veins.

'No,' she said coldly, 'I want nothing from you,' and

deliberately she unfastened the watch he had lent her from around her wrist and dropped it on his lap. 'Thank you for the loan of that,' she said, and was looking out of the window when he picked it up and slipped it into his pocket.

'I'll carry your case in for you,' he said when they reached her apartment. Her case was on the pavement and he stood beside her and made to reach for it.

Tully was nearer and picked it up herself. 'I'd rather you didn't,' she said. 'If Richard is in it will only make explanations more difficult if you come in with me.'

Yate shrugged, 'As you wish.'

'Goodbye,' said Tully, her face set as she went to move past him.

'Tully.' She halted, her back to him, not turning round. 'If you need help any time—will you come to me?'

Without speaking Tully had the last word as she ignored him and carried on walking. She had no idea why he had said that, but she wished he hadn't. She wanted to remember him as a cold unfeeling man, and that, added to her own observations over this weekend, told her he wasn't.

'What are you doing back?' Richard was home, thunderstruck to see her walk in with her suitcase.

'It's a long story,' she said. 'Howard and I agreed to disagree—and I don't want to talk about it.'

Richard could see from her pale, set face that she was upset, and for once in his life showed a sensitivity to her feelings she was glad about. 'All right, love,' he said quietly. 'You'll tell me when you're ready, I suppose. Sit down and I'll make you a cup of tea.'

True to this new-found sensitivity in him, or maybe because he couldn't stand Howard anyway, for the rest of the evening until it was time to go to bed, he didn't mention Howard's name. Though barely had Richard brought her the cup of tea he had promised than he was asking how she had got on Friday night.

Was it only Friday she had left here with anti-criminal

intent? It seemed like a lifetime away to her as Tully sketched an outline of what she had done, though when she came to the point of actually placing the money into the safe, here her story varied greatly with what had happened.

'I got a little panicky at that stage,' she told him, 'so I just bundled the money in, plastic bag and all.'

'Oh, hell—did you?' Richard asked, his face thoughtful, then brightening, 'Well, not to worry about that—I've got a reputation for being an untidy so-and-so, so apart from raising his eyebrows and praying to Allah, old Burgess won't think anything of it.'

'Sorry I dropped your keys,' Tully thought to add, only just remembering that was the excuse Yate had used when he had come to confront her brother.

'Fancy Mr Meachem finding them,' Richard remarked Then, 'Perhaps it's just as well he did, seeing you dropped them so near to the premises. If anyone else had found them and nipped in and helped themselves, my head would have been on the chopping block for sure.'

'Er—didn't you know he might be there?'

'Good lord no—Do you think I would have let you go if I had?'

'No—no, of course not,' Tully answered, recalling at the same time that Richard had forgotten to mention that the firm employed at least one security guard to her knowledge, though she couldn't mention that since she wasn't supposed to have seen anyone.

'It must have been sheer coincidence that he turned up shortly after you'd left—thank the lord he didn't show while you were there.'

'Amen to that,' said Tully, with an irony that was lost on Richard.

'Mr Meachem has other interests besides our firm,' Richard told her. 'He's always flying off to visit one or other of them. He'd probably just got back from one of his trips and took it into his head to fill in a few hours at the London office.'

'Probably,' Tully agreed. From what she had learned of Yate she knew, to say the least, that his methods were unorthodox. To him, starting on fresh work when everyone else had finished would more than likely seem normal.

She was up to see Richard off to work on Monday morning. She was on holiday, so could easily have stayed an extra hour in bed, but she felt restless, moody even, which was so unlike her, she thought some action would be the best antidote for it.

The whole day was spent in sprucing up the apartment. It needed it too, she thought ruefully. Two days on his own with no one to clear up after him and the place looked like a second-hand shop on sale day. But as hard as she worked, washing, polishing, tidying, preparing a meal for Richard when he came home, nothing could dispel the restlessness that had been with her from when she had first opened her eyes that morning, though she managed to have a cheerful smile on her face when she heard Richard's key in the door.

'Have a good day?' she greeted him, preparing to go into the kitchen to check on how the pie was doing in the oven.

'I'm not sure,' Richard said slowly.

'Not sure?' There was a serious look on Richard's face, and wondering if he was going to have one of his off moods, and not sure she could cope with it if he was because she didn't feel any too bright herself, Tully said, 'Just a minute, I'll go and turn the oven down, then you can tell me about it.'

It took only seconds for her to do the job she had come into the kitchen to do, but as Richard's uncertain answer played back in her mind, she felt the fingers of fear clutching at her. Had she left some other evidence lying about on Friday? Had Richard been questioned about it? She swallowed down her fear, it wouldn't do either of them any good, and surely Yate hadn't started a vendetta against Richard—that account had been paid. But when she did gather up her courage to go and face her brother, she learned that the account was very far from settled, though Richard in his ignorance of how badly things had gone awry last Friday fortunately hadn't put two and two together.

'It was about eleven o'clock,' he told her. 'I'd just finished doing the change over with old Burgess, left him getting the money ready for the armoured truck to call for the cash, when I get a message I'm wanted in Personnel.'

'Personnel?' Tully queried, her disquiet growing.

'Mm,' Richard assented. 'I hadn't asked for an interview, so I wondered what the deuce they wanted to see me about. Anyway, off I trotted to see Mr Payne. He's good at his job, I'll give him that, made me feel all relaxed and comfortable. Asked if I was married, questions like that—I could have got married without it showing on my record, I suppose. Anyway, that was just a lead-up question, I think, then he asked after my family—you know, parents, brothers and sisters, that sort of thing.'

Tully's anxiety was growing the longer Richard took to come to the point of his interview. But she didn't dare let it show and kept her hands out of sight so he shouldn't see they were trembling.

'I must have been with him for about an hour—it was as though he was really interested in me as a person, not just another cog to make the wheels go round, if you see what I mean. I really felt I could open up to him, he's one of those sort of people.'

'So you chatted,' Tully prompted. 'Told him a little about yourself ...'

'More than a little,' Richard said reflectively. 'Though as I said, he's good at his job, and he is. Not once did I see him stifling a yawn of boredom.'

'But what did he want to see you about?'

'Oh, the usual things. Was I happy doing the job I was doing?—Did I think I was cut out for doing cashier work?—that sort of thing.'

Daylight was beginning to filter through to Tully. She saw Yate Meachem's hand in all this. It couldn't be *just* coincidence, she was sure of it.

'So you told him you were,' she said, hoping her apprehension wasn't showing. 'You told him you were happy working with Mr Burgess.'

'Did I hell! Mr Payne seemed to want the truth, so I told him.'

'You told him?' Tully echoed dully, knowing for certain Richard had just said goodbye to any chances he might have of progressing further with the company.

'I did,' said Richard, not a bit abashed that Tully thought he had been tactless in the extreme. 'I told him straight, cashier work, being cooped up in an office, was driving me up the wall.'

'And what did he say to that?' Tully asked faintly.

'He asked me what I would like to do if given the choice —I really opened up then. Well, he wanted me to,' he explained as he saw she wasn't taking what he was telling her very well. 'He really did, Tully. I told him about the wine-making business I'd been all set to start until I found out our *beloved* stepfather had spent what was rightfully mine—ours,' he amended.

'You didn't—didn't tell him about Monty?'

'I did. Couldn't see any reason not to. I told him all about Monty stealing what was ours—how bitter I felt about it, and heaven knows what else I told him besides. I told you, Tully, Mr Payne really wanted to know.'

I'll bet he did, Tully thought, and everything you've told him will go straight back to Yate. Probably gone already. She couldn't begin to think what Yate would do with the information, but it was a foregone conclusion, distrusting Richard as he did, that he wouldn't want him having such easy access to the firm's money. This she was sure was the first step to getting him out, and Richard, lovable idiot though he was, had just jumped in with both feet.

Two days later, her suspicions that Yate intended to have Richard removed from his job in the cashiers department became fact, though she would never had guessed the way he had chosen to do it.

Since the apartment was already spick and span, just an hour or so's work after Richard had left that morning, Tully decided it was time she had some fresh air. She had worried constantly ever since her brother's disclosure of his interview with the personnel manager on Monday. She had fully expected him to come home last night saying he had been given his notice. But Richard had come home, if not exactly in a cheerful frame of mind, then no different from the way she had seen him dozens of times.

Perhaps she had it all wrong, she thought, as she grabbed up her shopping basket that Wednesday morning and went out. But that niggle of doubt, the constant knowledge that Yate didn't trust Richard, the thought that Yate, Yate as she knew him, just wouldn't have a person he didn't trust doing the work her brother was doing, was nudging at her elbow every minute of the day.

She was waiting to read in Richard's face any sign that the smallest thing had gone wrong when he pushed the door open that night. But one look at him as he stood there and threw his briefcase on to the settee told her she wouldn't have to *search* his face to see how his day had gone, for the grin he was wearing was stretching from ear to ear.

'Don't tell me, let me guess,' she said, her doubts and fears dwindling in face of the joy that was transparent in him. Then teasingly, 'They've offered you a seat on the board.'

'Better than that,' Richard retorted, then, the exuberance of his feelings too much to be contained, he came over, picked her up and swung her round. 'I'm going to France to be a trainee manager at one of Meachem's wine-making interests over there!'

The shock of her brother's announcement hadn't completely worn off when Tully went to bed that night. But once having comprehended that she had been right in thinking that Yate would get Richard away, and fast, from all the money his section handled, she was still gasping at the speed everything was going to move from then on. Apparently a trainee manager was urgently needed, and if it was all right with Richard, he had been asked if he was prepared to fly to France on Sunday, and be ready to start work on Monday.

'Monday!' Tully echoed. 'But th . . .'

'It can't come soon enough for me,' Richard told her, and she had never seen him in such high spirits. 'Anyway, having told Mr Payne how keen I was to do that sort of work, I definitely wasn't going to stall for more time and risk losing the only chance I'm likely to get of doing something I really want to do.'

In view of the excited light in his eyes, Tully didn't make any further protests. Looked at from Richard's point of view, it was the chance of a lifetime, and she knew since this was all he had ever wanted to do, that he would make a success of it. She forgot her own doubts and worries about why Yate Meachem should take this trouble with her brother—he could more easily have transferred him to one of the other departments—and concentrated on planning for Richard's departure. His laundry would have to be seen to, his . . .

'I say,' suddenly it seemed to occur to him that he hadn't given any thought to how she would fare without him there, 'you'll be all right, won't you?'

'Of course I will.' Tully's smile beamed at him. She had been sure he wouldn't go away without giving her some little thought, but there was no need for him to worry. She would miss him dreadfully, of course, but they would have split up anyway if she married Howard. If . . .?

'You'll be able to manage my half of the rent?' Richard asked, then answering his own question, 'You always were a good manager, Tully—I don't know how you do it.' There was nothing magic about it, she thought, it was a case of having to. 'Anyway,' Richard added, 'you'll be marrying Howard soon I expect. Er—you never said what your spat was about, but it wasn't anything very serious, was it?'

'No,' Tully told him, though remembering the way Howard had said 'Possibly' when she had said she would see him when he came back, she didn't think he would forgive her too easily.

'Good,' said Richard, that problem out of the way wanting to get back to his own plans. 'I expect Howard will be round here the minute he hits London.'

'I expect he will,' Tully agreed, though she wasn't very certain about that.

It shook her somewhat that when she went to bed that night she thought not at all of Howard, and only spasmodically about Richard, but the one man she couldn't get out of her mind was Yate Meachem. It was natural she should think of him, she told herself, when for the umpteenth time she turned over, sleep light years away. Yate Meachem, whether he knew it or not, had done the brother she loved so much one gigantic favour—there was no other earthly reason he should occupy so much of her thoughts.

CHAPTER NINE

IT was quiet without Richard. Tully came home from her first day back at work to a tidy apartment. It had been fortunate that she had been on holiday last week. Richard had asked her to sort through his things, and that in itself had been a mammoth task, for he was a hoarder and had old magazines by the dozens, neckties he would never wear, countless memories of life at Westover Rise. She had shed tears as she had come across the framed picture of her mother. There had been old snapshots of herself too, but nothing there at all to remind him of Monty. She hadn't realised quite how much Richard had hated Monty until she had come across a snap of her mother, remembered Monty had been in the picture too, but had been cut off.

As he had promised he would, Richard telephoned her that night, and she felt quite bright on hearing how happy he sounded, but that brightness didn't stay with her as the evening stretched on. Now that the rush and bustle of his departure was over, the apartment more or less immaculate, Tully felt lost, and for the first time, she experienced loneliness. Yate Meachem crept into her thoughts, but she pushed him firmly to the background. It wasn't him she was lonely for, for goodness' sake, ridiculous thought—no, it was Richard she was missing.

Her loneliness of spirit was still with her by the time Thursday came around. Howard must be back by now, and as she washed up her things from her early evening meal, Tully was sorely tempted to give him a ring. She decided against it, not sure why. She had rung him countless times in the past. She owed him a call, she argued with herself. It was up to her to try and put things right between them—

after all, it had been she who had messed up their holiday arrangements. But something stopped her from making that call, and when Yate forced himself to the forefront of her mind again, she thought perhaps it was because of the un-inhibited way she had reacted to his physical arousal of her, the guilt she had felt ever since that stopped her ringing Howard.

The washing up finished, ready to go in search of some-thing to read to keep her thoughts occupied until it was time to go to bed, Tully's footsteps in the direction of the book-case were halted by the sound of someone at her door. Her mind went over several people it could be—one of the girls from the office lived nearby and had said she might pop in to borrow one of her foreign language books if she couldn't find her own. Lindy had an exam coming and was studying like mad.

But it wasn't Lindy who stood there, but Howard. A Howard looking the same as ever—yet different. For the first time, as Tully said, 'Hello—come in,' she noticed a certain slackness about his mouth. She sent the thought on its way. She was pleased to see Howard—she was pleased to see anybody, the way her spirits were descending all the time.

'Did you have a nice holiday?' she asked, as Howard seated himself familiarly in his usual chair.

'Would have been better if you'd been there.' Tully didn't miss the accusation in his tone.

'I'm sorry, Howard,' she said, colouring as she remem-bered her lie. 'I'm sorry I couldn't come with you, but I just couldn't get out of it.' Well, that part was true. There had been no way Yate would have let her off the hook. Sud-denly, remembering Lindy might call, Tully knew a dread-ful anxiety in case Lindy should arrive and let drop that she hadn't been at work last week. Lindy had met Howard, knew they had been going on holiday together—it would be the most natural thing in the world for her to ask how they had got on. Tully recalled in answer to Lindy's enquiry on Monday of had she had a nice holiday, replying 'Super' and leaving it at that.

'Er—did you come for anything special, Howard?' she asked, trying to keep calm, and not missing his surprised look at the hint of a suggestion that it might have been better it he had telephoned first.

'I thought we'd got past the stage where I had to make a date to see you.'

'Yes—yes, of course we have—only I was—er—going to wash my hair tonight.' Oh dear, Howard was looking sulky. As well he might, she thought fairly. Hair washing as an excuse was the oldest one in the book.

'Surely you can wash it another night? It's two weeks since I saw you, for heaven's sake.'

'I was in on Monday,' Tully said pointedly. Tuesday and Wednesday for that matter, she thought, realising they were on the brink of a quarrel.

'I still wasn't feeling very friendly to you on Monday,' Howard said. 'You let me down badly, Tully.'

So he'd thought to let her stew? At any other time, she realised, that would have upset her, that he could love her and be so cruel, but now, strangely, she didn't feel hurt at all. Even thought perhaps, since he considered she had let him down badly, that he was justified in feeling the way he had, though the excuse she had given him had been a viable one.

'You're feeling more friendly to me now,' she said, and smiled because really she had no wish to quarrel with him.

'I missed you,' he said in answer, which gave her no indication whether he had forgiven her or not. 'I think we'd better get married Tully.'

His proposal, calm, unemotional, shattered her. She had been waiting, hoping just to hear those words, if not exactly phrased that way, then the outcome being the same. But what was more shattering was the bewildering thought that chased through her mind, I don't want to marry him. She looked at him, saw an averagely built man of twenty-eight, neither fat nor thin, and the thought was still there. After all her hopes, her plans, her longing for the day, she just didn't want to marry him. She didn't love him.

'You look funny—what's the matter?' His voice seemed to be coming from a long way off, and she forced herself to take in what he was saying. 'It can't be a surprise to you— you must have known we would get married some day. I would have preferred that my parents met you first, but there'll be time before the wedding.'

She had to stop him. He was taking her acceptance for granted. Guiltily she realised she had given him every encouragement to think that way. But as she looked at him, she knew she couldn't do it.

'I'm sorry Howard,' she said quietly, and wished she felt more adequate to deal with this situation. Restlessly she stood up. 'I'm sorry—I can't marry you.'

Howard stood up too, his face showing disbelief, amazement. 'What do you mean, you can't marry me? Of course you can! You've known all along we'd be married some day. I know I've never asked you, but you knew, you must have done.' He looked all set to say more in the same vein, but Tully knew if he badgered her from now until midnight her answer would still be the same.

'I'm sorry, Howard, really sorry,' she interrupted him. 'Everything you're saying is true, but I . . . I just don't want to marry you.'

'You're peeved because I left it until tonight to come round to see you,' he guessed, and before she could deny it or stop him he came over and put his arms around her.

She didn't want his arms about her, didn't want him to touch her, but she could not find it in her to hurt him further by pushing his arms away from her and rejecting him completely.

'I know what will put you right,' he said, as if thinking to sweeten her, and his head came down to kiss her as he had often before. But this time as his lips met hers, something within her recoiled. It seemed a violation that he should dare to kiss her lips, and she shrugged angrily away and out of his arms.

'Don't!' she said sharply, then stonily, 'I don't love you.' And as the words left her lips, like a blinding light coming through a pitch black tunnel, she realised just why, when the touch of Howard's lips was known to her, had been enjoyed before, why she had felt that revulsion when his mouth had met hers. She wasn't in love with Howard. She was in love with Yate Meachem, and it seemed indecent to be in any man's arms but his.

'You don't love me?' Howard's voice sounded incredulous, though Tully thought she was the one near to fainting with shock. 'But you told me you did—you said . . .'

'I thought I loved you,' her voice faded as she added, 'but I don't.'

Howard had been gone half an hour before Tully came out of her trancelike state. Howard had been furious and had really let rip into her. Phrases like, leading him on, letting him make a fool of himself, they all spun dizzily round in her head. And he was right, of course, she was everything he had said she was, had done everything he had said she had done, though she couldn't agree with his parting shot that she should be horsewhipped. She hadn't asked to fall in love with Yate. She didn't want to believe she had, but there was no getting away from it. It hurt, was painful like nothing else she had ever experienced—the love she thought she had felt for Howard was a lukewarm thing in comparison.

This, then, was the reason for her restlessness, her moody feelings. The reason Yate was constantly in her thoughts, the reason she had responded to his lovemaking without thought or care to where it had been leading. Given free choice Yate would have been the last man to whom she would have chosen to give her heart. Telling herself she didn't want to love him, couldn't be in love with a man who on his own admission had been in bed with his own brother's fiancée, wasn't any good. He didn't even have the excuse that he had been in love with Rowena—there had been little love in that heartfelt statement about 'that bitch Rowena having hysterics'. No, Tully thought, given the choice, Yate Meachem wouldn't figure at all—the pity of it was that when it came to falling in love, choice didn't enter into it.

Feeling despondent, dull, miserable, flat, all depressing adjectives fitting, Tully got up, wiped tears from her cheeks she hadn't known she had been shedding, and grasping at any small action that might oust her enervating thoughts, went into the kitchen to make herself a hot drink. The front door bell went twice before she heard it. She came out of the kitchen, glanced at the clock on the mantelpiece, saw it was nine-thirty, and the thought passed through her mind that Lindy was going to be up all night if she was only now getting down to do her studying. Knowing Lindy would be in a tearing hurry, Tully took the book she had promised to loan her with her.

The lighthearted words she had prepared to say as she thrust the book into Lindy's hands disappeared, as the door opened and Tully saw the doorway filled with the over-powering figure of the man who had occupied all her thoughts ever since Howard had gone. Yate stood there, his eyes going over her jeans and sweater-clad body to return to her face and favour her with an expression that said he had taken in that she had been crying.

'I thought you were a friend coming to borrow this,' she said foolishly, pulling back the book she had been about to thrust into his hands.

Yate looked down at the title. 'Can't say that it's one that I've read,' he said sardonically. 'May I come in?'

'Yes, yes, of course.' Tully stood back. She knew she

should have said, no, no, a hundred time no, but his reminder that her manners were at fault, coupled with the fact that she wanted him with her, had her stepping back from the door to allow him to enter, before it came to her that he hadn't dropped in to see her on a casual visit.

'Richard,' she said hastily, as he closed the door and walked into the room. 'Nothing's wrong with Richard, is there?'

'How you women jump to conclusions! Your brother is fine as far as I know.'

'Oh—er . . .'

'Why have you been crying?'

She should have known his eagle eyes missed very little. 'I've just made some coffee, would you like a cup?' She needed a few minutes alone in the kitchen to get herself under control. And he couldn't really be interested in why she had been crying anyway, though she hadn't thought he would let her get away with not answering him.

'I'd love a cup,' he accepted. 'I've just left the office and there are few things I'd appreciate more.'

Tully stood in the kitchen doorway for a second, his coffee in her hand. She had thought she had herself under control, but her senses went all haywire just to see the back of his fair head as he sat on the settee. He turned his head and saw her standing there, so she had to move if she didn't want him to know she had been watching him.

'Do you work until this hour every night?' she asked, thinking it a nice safe topic and handing him his coffee at the same time before taking the seat opposite him.

'Lord, no! I've been away for a while and only looked in to clear up a few odds and ends that appeared urgent.'

That was the end of that conversation, and she searched around in her mind for something else to say that would get her through the time until he was ready to reveal his reason for calling. One just didn't push people like Yate, he would tell her when he was ready and not before. Besides which, she didn't want him to go, not just yet, she thought, and didn't care that she was being foolhardy. Sense flew out of the window when love flew in.

'Th-thank you for what you've done for Richard,' she said, even if Yate's reasons for getting her brother away from the London office were not quite what everyone else would believe; he needn't have done what he had.

'You don't have to thank me.'

'Yes, I do,' she contradicted him. 'I know why you did it—know you wanted him out of the cashier's office, but you could have done that without finding him the one job he wanted above all others. He was thrilled to bits with the chance you've given him of going to France and ...'

'Is that why you were crying—because you're lonely here on your own?'

'Oh no, I'm too happy for him to cry now that he's gone. I miss him, of course,' she said, and smiled. 'I'm so used to tidying up after him ...'

'You're not a girl who cries easily, Tully?' Yate probed.

He wasn't prepared to go away without finding the reason for her tears, it seemed, but Tully knew that nothing was going to drag from her that her tears had been on account of realising how deeply she loved him, this man who now looked determined to get to the root of what had caused her tears to flow. She firmed her lips together. Perhaps if Yate got tired of waiting he would get round to telling her why he was here.

'Would I be right in thinking you're feeling dejected because the boy-friend's "possibly" in connection with seeing you again, meant, "Never"?' he asked after some moments' thought. So he had remembered what he had overheard of her telephone conversation? She allowed herself a small smile. Yate was successfully following the wrong track.

'Howard was here tonight, as a matter of fact,' she said, and hoped she didn't sound too smug at leading him away from the real reason she had cried.

'He didn't stay long, did he? Do I take it that he's not prepared to forgive you for daring to work when you should have been on holiday? Were your tears on account of his writing "finis" to your romance?'

It annoyed her that Yate didn't sound as if he cared a jot, when had that been Howard's reason for leaving so early, it would have been all his fault for making her cancel her holiday arrangements anyway.

'For your information, Howard asked me to marry him.' Oh, how she wished her spurt of temper hadn't egged her on to let him know that snippet of knowledge. 'I didn't mean to tell you that,' she said.

Yate accepted that his probing had her telling him what she would have wanted to remain private between her and Howard, but it didn't stop his badgering questioning.

'From the look of you I hardly think you've been weeping out of sheer, sublime happiness?'

'I . . . I turned him down. I . . .'

'You turned him down? I thought you were in love with the chap?'

'So did I.' Oh, how she wanted to change the subject, he had her so confused she was saying all the wrong things. Any minute now Yate would start wondering since she had once told him she hoped to marry Howard what had happened to make her change her mind. 'Can we drop this?' she asked, doubting that he would if he didn't feel like it.

'Howard didn't take his marching orders very well?' Yate didn't sound as if the thought of a rejected Howard was anything to lose any sleep over, in fact his voice sounded as though he fully endorsed what she had done. His voice, she was sure, had a touch of humour to it as he asked, 'Did he go off in a huff?'

Yate had the darnedest way of swinging her emotions right around and upside down; she almost felt like grinning suddenly at his suggestion of Howard going off in a huff, for that was pretty much the way Howard had gone.

'He said I should be horsewhipped,' she said, a feeling of being much more able to cope coming over her.

'Very loverlike, I'm sure,' said Yate, and she just had to look at him to see if he was smiling. He wasn't smiling, but his eyes had lost that hard glint, and he looked much more approachable.

'Yes—well, you didn't come here to talk about Howard,' she hinted.

Yate was in no hurry to tell her why he had called. He finished off his coffee and set his cup down on a small table before he looked directly at her and said:

'I want to go down to the Grange this weekend.' He paused, then not taking his eyes off her, said deliberately, 'Will you come with me?'

Tully was on her feet, her back towards him without her knowing she had risen. She couldn't go with him, she couldn't. It would be much too painful.

'I ... I thought our account was settled—thought by coming with you that other time I'd paid for ...' Her voice tailed off, but she nearly jumped out of her skin when she heard his voice coming from directly over her shoulder. She hadn't heard him move.

'The account is settled, Tully. I'm not forcing you to come with me—I'm asking if you will.' She felt his hands come down lightly on her shoulders, didn't want to turn and face him, but had no choice in the matter as he pulled her round and looked down at her. 'Will you, Tully? Will you come with me?'

She realised then exactly why he was asking her. Yate was so concerned that Bart should walk again he thought her being with him would make Bart feel more secure with Jackie. That Yate had not shown the slightest interest in Jackie other than a natural friendliness any man would have towards a future sister-in-law was neither here nor there. Bart had been deeply wounded by Yate's carrying on with his ex-fiancée. She knew then she would go, though she was honest enough to face that it wasn't for Bart's sake that she would go, much as she too would like to see him walk. She would go because Jackie had said Yate had always protected his brother, and Yate must be hurting like hell inside that his thoughtless action had resulted in Bart being crippled.

She looked into Yate's unwavering blue gaze. 'I'll come,' she said quietly, and had the hardest work in the world to keep her hands to her sides when Yate's grip on her shoulders tightened fractionally and he bent to bestow a gentle kiss on her mouth.

Time and again in the hours remaining before Yate called for her the following evening, Tully told herself she was a fool. She should have said no. Bart would walk again, the doctors had said he would. Her going wasn't going to make any difference, she told herself over and over, yet each time the memory of the affection Yate had for Bart would trip her up and she didn't so much as look Yate up in the phone book in order to ring and say she wouldn't go after all. That grin she had seen Yate and Bart exchange had been full of what they must have been like before the business of Rowena, and try as she might, she couldn't fathom what had got into Yate to do what he had done. He was a virile man, she herself was only too fully aware of that, but his brother's fiancée? When he thought so much of Bart?

Telling herself she would be cool and calm when next she saw Yate, had been another wasted exercise, for her heart began fluttering alarmingly when she heard him at her door, and that was before she had even seen him. He was dressed in a well fitting business suit of a pinstripe grey, and she felt the usual confused gamut of emotions rage through her as she bade him come in.

'I'm ready,' she said, 'I'll just check the apartment.' Then realising he must have come straight from the office, 'Would you like something to eat—a drink of anything before we go?'

'Thanks, no. It won't take us long and I expect Evie will have something prepared for us when we get there.'

Tully's intention was to speak only when spoken to whenever they were alone. Her intention to be aloof, guarded and never to allow that guard to drop, had been so much pie in the sky, she realised, as once they had left London behind, Yate started up a conversation, and for all it was impersonal, there was none of the coldness in him she had witnessed on the two previous occasions she had driven with him. And the further on they went, sometimes talking, sometimes not, she felt a bubbling happiness growing within her that scattered her reserve to the four winds. Yate was no longer treating her like a criminal, but as an equal.

Evie was in the hall to greet them. 'I've a table laid for you,' she said, her special smile for Yate much in evidence. 'Mrs Meachem and Mr Bart are in the drawing room. Miss Jackie can't get here until tomorrow.'

'We'll leave our cases here and go and say hello first, I think,' Yate told her. 'We'll eat in about fifteen minutes, all right with you, Evie?'

'Yes, of course. I'll have your cases taken up.'

It felt like a proper homecoming to Tully, and her happiness grew at the warm welcome she and Yate received from Mrs Meachem and Bart. 'Jackie can't get here until tomorrow,' Bart told them as Evie had done. 'They're stocktaking or some such where she works. Still,' he said cheerfully, 'Jackie will be allowed time off in lieu, so she'll be here for a long weekend next weekend.'

Tully was thrilled to note in the few minutes' talk that followed that the animosity that had been only just beneath the surface between Yate and his brother the first time she had seen them together was now a thing of the past.

'We'd better go and have something to eat or we'll be in Evie's black books,' Yate said after about five minutes. 'Do you want to go up to your room first, Tully?'

'I'll wash my hands . . .'

'Come on, then.'

She liked the feel of his arm at the back of her waist as they left the room, loose though his hold was. But as she would have gone towards the staircase that led to the west wing the grip at her waist tightened, bringing her to a halt.

'This way,' said Yate, his tone sounding cool, and some of her happiness diminished as she looked up at him, saw his look was as cool and remote as his voice as he said, 'I hope you don't mind, we've given you a different room this time.'

'Not at all.' Her voice was as cool as his as his arm dropped away and she went with him up the main staircase where he showed her into a bedroom similar to the one she had expected to occupy in the west wing.

'I'll see you in the dining room in about five minutes.' He seemed to hesitate, and Tully hoped with all her heart it wasn't because her bewilderment was showing. 'You'll be all right here?'

'Why, of course,' she said, glad she had been able to inject a note of surprise that he should think anything other.

'Good,' he said shortly, and left her.

Oh, what a fool she was! There had been nothing in any way personal in Yate's manner. Ever since he had called for her at the apartment it had been almost as if he had been at pains to keep everything between them strictly impersonal. She didn't have to look further than the fact that he wanted her sleeping as far away from him as possible to know that. To think she had been looking forward to going to the west wing, to know he was near, would have been enough. But oh, how utterly devastating to know that to serve his purpose, that purpose of letting Bart know Jackie was completely safe from him because he had his own girl-friend, Yate Meachem, not liking her, not trusting her, was prepared to put aside the knowledge of what he termed her sticky fingers and bring her to his home only for his brother's sake.

Swallowing hard, she faced the fact that she was an idiot. She had known last night when Yate had asked her to come with him that his invitation had been solely on account of Bart—anything else had been just wishful thinking on her part. Yet it hurt to have it rammed home to her this way, hurt to know that Yate didn't like her. Briefly he had desired her—but his desire for her had little to do with liking.

Determined not to cry, Tully went into the adjoining bathroom and washed her hands. Her make-up needed little attention as she had made up freshly before Yate had called for her. This time her resolve to be cool, calm and collected, wouldn't waver, she thought as she left her room and made for the dining room. Armed with the painful knowledge that she had been living in cloud cuckoo land to have imagined for one instant that Yate had begun to like her a little, her pride was up in arms that he was just using her, though, in all fairness, he had never suggested anything else.

She knew as the meal progressed that Yate had observed the change in her manner towards him, she had caught the way his eyebrows had ascended slightly when her napkin had slid on to the floor and they had both gone to retrieve it. She had snatched it up, knocking her hand against the table in her anxiety, afraid his hand might touch hers and set off that alarming, quivering yearning that only he could arouse in her.

'Did you hurt yourself?'

'No-no,' Tully replied quickly. The stinging would go off in a moment.

And then suddenly it dawned on her, as he sat watching her, knowing she would dearly love to give her bruised knuckle a good rub, that since she had shown him clearly he didn't matter a hoot to her, honour redeemed, she didn't want him to get the idea she was piqued if, with his astute brain, he started to reason that she had been much more natural with him until he had told her she would be sleeping in another room. She would have to change course again, she thought, feeling not unlike a chameleon.

'Have you been busy this week?' she asked brightly, and saw from his quick look that he must be thinking she changed her personality with every breath.

'Done my share, I think,' he said. 'Shall we join Mother and Bart in the drawing room?'

In the company of Mrs Meachem and Bart, Tully found the need to be on her guard with Yate fading. She didn't feel very loverlike towards him, but should her unwary heart show through her strict control, then since she was acting the part of letting everyone think she thought he was the grestest thing since the invention of the wheel, Yate would think it was all part of the act.

She felt less inhibited with Bart, as he teased her about being a blue-stocking when in answer to his mother's question of how many languages was she fluent in, she had answered four.

'Not at all,' she protested. 'It was sheer hard plod to get passes in other subjects. It's only languages I pick up easily.'

She saw then that Yate had been watching this piece of nonsense, and smiled at him in case anyone was watching, though her spirits sank to zero as the thought struck her that he must be silently refuting her statement; hadn't he caught her in the act of picking up his money?

'You can prove that statement. Come and let me beat you at chess,' Bart said. 'I'd ask Yate to play, but he always beats me hollow. You can play chess?' he thought to ask.

'Yes—I used to play with Monty.'

'Monty?' Bart queried, and looked at Yate as though suspecting she had a boy-friend his brother didn't know about.

'Monty was Tully's stepfather,' Yate told him.

Tully knew for sure then that Mr Payne, the personnel manager at Meachem's, had related word for word to him everything Richard had told him, because she was certain she had never breathed Monty's name to anyone in the room. She recalled clearly when she had been telling Mrs Meachem something of her family the last time she had been here, that she had referred to Monty as her stepfather only. Her glance met Yate's. Met and held. He knew what was going through her mind, she was sure of it, but her eyes were the first to drop away.

Bart beat her at chess. He probably would have done anyway, Tully thought, even had she been concentrating on the game, and by no stretch of the imagination had she been doing that. She was conscious all the time of the quiet conversation going on in the background between Yate and his mother, conscious that occasionally his eyes would flick in her direction, but she hadn't looked at him to try and gauge what if anything those glances meant.

'You're too good for me,' Tully told Bart, laying down her king.

'Care for the equaliser?' He looked at his watch. 'Is that the time? I should be in bed getting my beauty sleep.'

'You should never have got up,' Tully teased him as she would have done Richard, knowing he wouldn't take offence since she had told him the first time she had seen him that he was better looking than Yate.

Bart gave a shout of laughter. 'Did you hear that, Yate—you're going to have your work cut out handling this one!'

'Don't I know it,' Yate said pleasantly, and strolled over to drop his arm lightly across her shoulders.

'I think I'll go to bed if nobody would mind,' said Tully, controlling the impulse to place her hand over Yate's as it rested on her.

'I'll see you to the bottom of the stairs,' he said, and she couldn't see why he should bother until she realised, of course, if she said goodnight to him in this room he would be expected to give her a peck on the cheek at least.

His arm fell away as she rose to her feet, saying goodnight to Mrs Meachem and Bart. She walked to the door, found Yate there to open it for her, and told herself to keep calm. Yate went with her to the bottom of the stair-case. She turned, intending to offer a quick 'Goodnight' and to get away from his disturbing presence.

'Thank you, Tully,' he said unexpectedly.

'What for?' She couldn't see why he was thanking her. 'Oh, you mean coming with you? That's ...'

'No, not just that. Thank you for being so natural with Bart. Jackie was telling me that people generally have an uncanny knack of treating anyone in a wheelchair as though they have two heads—you're more sensitive than that, aren't you?'

Tully felt helpless; she didn't know what to say. And then, when all evening she had taken trouble to keep Yate from knowing how she felt about him, she witnessed in his eyes that his brother's pain was his pain, and something in her she couldn't control took over, and it was instinctive to stretch up and place a gentle kiss on his mouth.

Panic at what she had done took over, and as Yate's hands came to grip tightly on her arms she wrenched herself out of his grasp and fairly flew up the stairs, not daring to look back, not stopping, her heart pounding, though not from running up the stairs, until she was safely in her room. She turned the key in the lock, and didn't know why she had, because Yate didn't follow her.

CHAPTER TEN

CONTRARY to her expectations, Tully slept well that night. She was glad when Marian brought in a tray of early morning tea that she'd had second thoughts and had unlocked her door before slipping into bed. She would hate Marian to speculate why she had found it necessary to lock her door, and maybe discuss it with the rest of the staff.

Sliding out of bed, Tully went to the window, looking out beyond the well-tended gardens to the fields beyond and wondering what today would bring. She wanted this weekend to be without a flaw, to be something she would remember for the rest of her life. Yate had been so impersonal with her last night when they had been on their own. It was the only way, of course, and she would follow his lead. He mustn't be allowed to harbour the faintest suspicion of how she felt about him, yet it grieved her that he had no warmth for her. Oh, he had put his arm around her shoulders when she had finished her game of chess with Bart, but that had been purely because Bart had been there and the role they were acting. She remembered what she had been trying to forget since she had first opened her eyes—how could she have been so crass as to kiss him?

Not wanting to dwell on that kiss, the feel of his lips warm beneath her own, she hurried to the bathroom. Twenty minutes later, dressed in jeans and a snug fitting T-shirt, she made her way to the breakfast room. Nothing had been said of what they were going to do today, but if Yate had anything planned, she could easily run up to her room and change. If he had nothing in mind, she would go for a walk on her own. A small sigh escaped her; she was so in love with him she was eager to fall in with anything he had to suggest. It required a deep breath before she opened the door of the breakfast room, but totally not needed, as her first glance showed that only Bart was there.

'Don't look so disappointed,' he said cheerfully, making her realise she would have to take herself sternly in hand if it was so obvious she had expected to see Yate there. 'Though I think I know how you feel—Jackie affects me the same way,' Bart added with such understanding she almost felt like confiding in him, but she wouldn't of course.

'Brother Yate has had breakfast, he seemed restless and is out somewhere, so come and join me—we can console each other until our better halves arrive.' Bart was back to being teasing and Tully smiled at his remark as she sat down, wishing above all else to have Yate as her other half.

'Have you anything planned for this morning?' Bart enquired after commenting that she would never grow to be a strapping wench if she only ever ate toast for breakfast.

'I don't know—I was waiting to see what Yate ...'

'Got you where he wants you, has he?—That's what I like to see,' Bart tormented her, then seriously, 'I've got an errand to do at one of the farms. Yate said he was interested to see over the estate—if you like, when Jackie gets here, we can all go.'

'I'd like that,' Tully said simply, and her heart jumped into her mouth when she heard a sound of someone coming through the door behind her. It could have been one of the maids come to check if they wanted any more of anything, but Tully knew it wasn't even before she turned her head.

'Good morning, Tully,' Yate smiled at her, and as colour rioted through her face as she recalled the way she had impulsively kissed him last night, the smile on his face lit his eyes. Then the confusion only he could wreak on her wayward senses threatened to get completely out of hand as he bent his head and kissed her briefly on the mouth. It was purely because Bart was sitting there watching, she knew that, but her colour rose even higher when Yate said softly, 'I owed you that one.'

Unable to look at him, she flicked a glance at Bart. If she had expected Bart to look embarrassed at what she told herself sternly was only a piece of play-acting for his benefit anyway, then she was completely mistaken, for he looked highly delighted at this piece of byplay.

'I'm off,' he said, manipulating his wheelchair away from the table. 'See you later.'

Bart had told her Yate had already eaten, but instead of leaving her to finish her coffee as she supposed he would once Bart had gone, Yate unhooked one of the chairs from beneath the table and sat down, his fingers idly drumming on the tablecloth.

Tully stared as though fascinated at those long fingers on his man-sized hand. She felt tension in the air and wondered if it came solely from her—if she hadn't known better she would have said there was something nervous in the way Yate's fingers were beating on the table. She could have laughed at the thought if she hadn't felt so churned up inside. Yate nervous, a scoffing voice taunted her, that would be the day—she had never met a man so full of self-possession.

Then the fingers ceased their tattoo, and as though compelled Tully lifted her eyes from that hand and looked straight into serious blue eyes. Her glance flicked to his stern mouth, and suddenly the tension between them stretched, seemed to tauten to breaking point so that she was hard put to it not to swallow. It was as though something momentous was about to happen and she was outside looking in. Then Yate spoke, his voice gravelly as though he had a lot to say but was unsure where to begin.

'I have to talk to you, Tully,' he said slowly, as though each word had to be controlled.

'Y-yes, Yate.' He was so very serious, stern almost, and

her heart beat frantically against her rib cage as she wondered what was coming.

'I . . .' he began, and it was complete and utter anti-climax when before he could get any further, the door opened and Evie stood there.

Whether Evie felt the tension in the room Tully didn't know, but the sharp frown that descended on Yate's brow must have told her her interruption was most untimely. It caused her to say apologetically anyhow, 'There's a call for you from Stuttgart, Mr Yate,' and when Yate made no move to go, 'It sounds urgent.'

'All right, Evie.' Yate's brow cleared as he looked at the housekeeper's anxious face. 'I'll take it in the study.'

'I'll have the call transferred,' Evie said as she bustled away.

Yate stood up. 'I'd better go and see what's so urgent,' he said. 'Don't disappear, Tully, we'll find somewhere private for our talk.'

Tully sat frozen when he had gone, her mind going over countless possibilities of why he should want to have a talk with her. A serious talk, by the look of it. Richard was her first thought before she rejected it. No, it couldn't be Richard, could it? Richard had telephoned her on his first day in his new job and had said everything was great with a capital G. Richard wouldn't be handling money, would he, and since he was so keen to make a go of his job, he wouldn't risk losing it by doing anything stupid. Bart was her next thought, but she was at a loss to know why Yate should want to talk to her about Bart. By being here this weekend she was helping in every way she knew where Bart was concerned.

Marian coming to clear away made her realise she was holding up the household routine. 'Oh, I'm sorry,' said the shy Marian as she stood hesitating in the doorway, looking ready to bolt. 'I thought . . .'

'That's all right, Marian, come in,' Tully bade her. 'I was just leaving.'

Tully wandered along the hall, paused by the study door, heard Yate's voice firm and authoritative, and thought from the sound of it he would be some minutes yet. He had told her not to disappear, and since she couldn't wait in the breakfast room, he probably hadn't meant her to take him so literally anyway, the only other alternative was the drawing room, she thought.

Still pondering on what it was Yate had to talk to her about, Tully opened the drawing room door. Opened the door and halted, her eyes growing big in her face, a smile breaking across her face at the sight that met her. For there by the settee, his wheelchair some paces behind him, *stood* Bart. His shoulders were stooped as they had never been when he was sitting in his chair, but stooped as though he wasn't quite sure of himself, a look on his face exultant yet tentative, as though he wasn't quite sure what had happened. Then he looked across at her, and several things happened at once.

'I walked,' he said, then yelled at her, 'I walked four steps!' and as if he didn't believe it and had to convince himself, 'I walked four bloody steps!' then his confidence seemed to topple away from him and he started to fall.

Quick as lightning Tully flew from the doorway and caught him as he lurched over. Though not as large or as tall as Yate, Bart was heavy and his weight knocked the breath out of her as they fell, arms and legs all over the place, into the settee.

'Have you hurt yourself?' Tully gasped as soon as she had some breath back.

'Who the hell cares—I walked Tully, I walked!'

'Oh, Bart!' Tully felt tears surge to her eyes at the joy in him. She was oblivious to the fact that Yate had just that second come to stand in the doorway, his eyes taking in that his brother had his arms around her, and was lying half on top of her. 'Oh, my dear Bart,' Tully said softly, and because her own joy for him knew no bounds and his cheek was so near, she kissed him, a kiss she would have given her own brother in the same circumstances.

A sound by the door had both their heads turning in that direction. About to tell Yate the exciting news, it came to Tully that this was Bart's show, let him tell Yate and watch that stony look disappear from his face, she thought. Then she immediately realised that Yate's look wasn't stony, it was livid, furious, as mad as hell—and yet didn't he look hurt too?

'Yate,' said Bart, but he was talking to an empty doorway, for Yate turned smartly and strode out of their vision.

'What ...?' said Tully, her joy for Bart disappearing at the never-to-be forgotten look that had been on Yate's face.

Bart seemed as puzzled as her for a moment, then using his incredibly strong arms, made doubly strong by the use they had in levering himself in and out of his chair, he prised himself away from her, and realised how they must have looked to anyone standing in the doorway.

'Oh, my God,' he breathed. 'Oh, my God, no!'

'What is it?' Tully asked, wriggling herself from under him and sitting on the drawing room carpet. 'What was all that about?'

'History repeating itself—with a twist, I shouldn't wonder,' said Bart, and looking suddenly joyous again, though with a more happier light than before showing in his face if that was possible. 'History repeating itself,' he said again, as if only then something had made itself clear to him. 'What an ass I've been all this time,' he said, to her mystification. 'Though I've a feeling that that over-protective brother of mine has been an even bigger ass.'

Tully had thought Yate had the power to confuse her more than any man she knew, but Bart was running a very close second, she thought.

'Push my wheelchair over here, there's a love,' Bart was bidding her urgently. 'I've got to see Yate.'

Tully stood up, but as her hands reached the wheelchair she saw Yate go striding furiously past the window. 'Yate has gone out,' she said. 'He's just gone past the window.'

'He's not gone towards the garages, has he?' Bart rapped out.

'No—I don't think so.' Tully went to the window, sensing Bart's frustration that he couldn't get there himself. She could still see Yate, but the distance he had already put between himself and the house told her he wasn't hanging about. 'He's walking towards the fields,' she relayed to Bart.

'Thank God for that,' Bart said on a heartfelt sigh. 'At least he's not driving anywhere.'

Tully turned from the window, saw Bart had levered himself into a sitting position. She wheeled his chair nearer to him, but sensing his independence, stood to one side while he swung himself into it, and only when this had been achieved did she ask one of the questions that were fighting for precedence in her mind.

'What's going on, Bart?' she asked, her bewilderment obvious.

'You don't know?' Bart questioned in return, and seeing she hadn't got any idea, said soothingly, which was no help at all, 'Don't worry about a thing, Tully, nothing very dreadful has happened.'

'But——' she started to protest, then saw that Bart could at times be very much like his brother.

'Don't fret, Tully, there's a good child. Things have happened in this house that Yate has decided, wisely or unwisely, not to tell you about.' He tried to get a smile out of her. 'Far be it from me to go against one of Yate's decisions, though he wants his head examined for what he's let me think all ...' he broke off. 'Chin up, Tully, everything's going to be all right.'

Bart was not to be budged, and seeing this side of him,

Tully knew she was wasting her time. And then Jackie arrived, so after greeting the other girl and assuming that since Yate had stormed off and with Bart being so secretive and saying he wanted to see Yate before he went anywhere, the journey round the estate was off, Tully went up to her room hoping that once she was alone she might be able to come up with a few answers herself.

An hour later she didn't at all like the answers she had been able to come up with. It was all too clear now that Yate had seen her and Bart all tangled up together on the settee, but had no idea of the excitement that had gone on before because he had no idea Bart had walked. With a sick feeling inside her, she had realised that Yate had thought she and Bart were on the way to becoming lovers. That he hadn't liked what he had seen was obvious. His anger, it was patently clear now, had all been because he thought she was making a play for his brother. She had learned that the Grange belonged to Yate, but Bart had his own half share of the fortune left to him by his father. And Yate, distrusting her as he did, must suspect, since her one attempt at getting some easy money had come unstuck, that she was now after Bart for what she could get out of him.

She might just as well pack her case and leave, Tully considered. She couldn't take any more. Loving Yate, knowing he would never love her, but hoping at least that by playing the part of being his loving girl-friend the memory of what he thought he knew of her would fade and he might begin to think well of her—if he thought of her at all, she added with a cynicism that was growing in her—was all much too much.

About to take down her suitcase and begin packing the few things she had brought with her, Tully stopped, and hated the weakness in her that loving Yate brought. The love for him that pushed aside her feelings of injured pride and said she couldn't go like this, couldn't go until she had attempted to clear herself in his eyes. He wouldn't believe her, of course, but her mind was made up; she owed it to herself as much as to him to stay and face him. She had never run away from anything in her life, she wasn't about to start now. She hadn't been able to explain about that money, never would be able to if Richard was to be protected, but this *was* something she could explain.

Tully left her room. She suspected that Yate wasn't back yet, his stride had looked furious enough to get him to Land's End before he would realise how far he had gone. But she would sit in the drawing room and wait for him to go by the window.

Her intention to try and clear herself to Yate took a sideways dip as she saw him tightlipped with Bart in the hall. Bart saw her and smiled encouragingly, but Yate ignored her.

'We'll go into the study,' Yate said grimly, and strode off to leave Bart following behind.

The study door closed, and Tully found her feet taking her to the staircase that led to the west wing. Without conscious thought her feet mounted the stairs, and she was in the private sitting room without being fully aware of how she had got there. She opened the door to the bedroom she had slept in, saw Yate's hairbrushes reposing on the dressing table and knew he had slept in there last night. Silently she closed the door, returning to the sitting room to sink down on the settee.

She would go soon, must go before Yate came anywhere near. Though, she reflected, there couldn't be anywhere in the house that was more private than this for the talk he had wanted to have with her. A humourless smile tilted the corners of her mouth. That talk would be cancelled now. From the look on Yate's face, the way he had just cut her dead, there wasn't a thing he wanted to say to her. Restlessly she stood up and went to stare unseeingly out of the window. She might as well pack and go after all, she reasoned. Bart had walked four steps, it wouldn't be much longer before he was walking normally, his shoulders back. Anyway, what was she waiting here for? Bart would be telling Yate everything that had happened this morning, and the scene he had witnessed would fade into the background once Bart had told him he had walked. What Bart had meant by history repeating itself was still something she couldn't unravel—it must be something private between him and Yate.

Her unseeing eyes became aware of movement in the grounds below her, and pulling her gaze nearer to the house she focussed on the two people there. With a horrified exclamation, she realised it was Jackie and Bart.

It was so peaceful in the west wing, in contrast to her busy thoughts, she had lost all track of time. Yate and Bart must have left the study—oh, lord, she had been up here far too long. She turned swiftly intending to go quickly from the room, then her eyes widened, her breath left her on a strangled gasp. For there, having entered the room while she had been too deep in thought to have heard the door open, and as silently close, stood Yate with a look on his face that told her she wasn't going anywhere until he had said a few well-chosen words to her.

'I . . .' Tully struggled for words that would explain what she was doing in his private apartment. But none came. 'I . . . I'd better go,' she said, and started to walk towards him, only to stop dead when he made no move to step away from the door. He looked dangerous, too dangerous for her to put herself within arm's reach. He advanced a step, and it was a signal for Tully to take two paces backwards.

'Set this to music and we could have a new dance,' Yate said smoothly as he took another step towards her and she retreated yet again.

'Let me go, Yate,' she said, striving to make her voice sound normal.

'I didn't invite you to my parlour,' he said, his voice unhurried, 'but since you're here, you are going nowhere until I have a few answers.'

'D-didn't Bart explain about . . .'

'About you being in his arms, about the pair of you looking as though you were glued to each other and liking it that way? Yes, he explained.'

Tully had no idea why, with Bart having told him everything, Yate should still look so grim. 'Aren't you pleased that Bart can walk?—I thought you'd be delighted.'

'Of course I'm pleased, and more delighted than you can possibly know. I've waited for almost a year for this day, despaired at times of it ever coming.'

'Th-then why are you looking so grim?' she asked, her glance flicking to the door as Yate took another step towards her and she found her retreat blocked by the settee.

'Am I looking grim, Tully?' He took the other step that brought him close enough to touch her, but his hands stayed loosely at his sides, she was glad to note, while her insides churned over at his nearness. 'If I'm looking grim it's because we still have to have our talk, Tully, and I have no idea yet of the outcome.'

'Oh.' It was happening again as she knew it would. He was making her all confused. Her thoughts were getting mixed up with that scene he had witnessed between her and Bart that morning, and the way he had told her in the breakfast room that he wanted to talk to her.

'You haven't been thinking that I . . . I've been setting my cap at Bart, have you?' It must be that, she saw clearly now. He must have imagined even before seeing her in Bart's arms that she was after him and had been going to have a word with her about it. She remembered her teasing remarks to Bart, calling him better looking than Yate, and other stupid things she had said without thought. Whatever Bart had told him about his falling and her trying to catch him hadn't made Yate believe she hadn't tried to make capital out of the incident. 'It's true what Bart told you,' she said, growing angry that he could think so of her. 'He would have fallen if I hadn't caught him.'

'And you just couldn't help kissing and calling him your *dear*, I suppose.'

If it had been anyone but Yate, she would have suspected, even while overjoyed that his brother could walk again, that Yate was scorchingly jealous as he remembered the scene. That in itself was a laugh. Yate jealous—they'd have green snow on that day!

'No, I couldn't, if you want to know,' she flared, goaded on by the knowledge that she would never be able to arouse his jealousy. 'You weren't there to see the look on Bart's face just before he started to fall. If it's possible for a man to look radiant, Bart was radiant. His confidence slipped and I only just got to him in time to cushion his fall. It was like holding my own brother in my arms—the kiss was an impulse on the sheer joy of the moment.' She would like to have added, 'So there,' but held it back, knowing it would sound childish.

'So you have no interest in Bart apart from—sisterly feelings?'

Stubbornly Tully kept her mouth closed. She had been right then, even if the reason he wanted to talk to her had come to her a little late. She felt hurt, wounded, and wished now she had followed her first impulse and packed her case and left.

'I'll go,' she said, her temper leaving her as the misery of her thoughts defeated it. 'Bart will walk now—there's no need for me to be here any longer.' She made to walk round him, not thinking he would stop her, but his hand came out before she had got to the side of him.

'And what about our talk, Tully? What about that?'

Her head came up, and she stared into his hard blue eyes. 'W-wasn't that it?' Oh, damn this way he had of making a nonsense of her thought processes!

'That,' said Yate meaningfully, 'was just clearing away a few frayed ends. We have yet to get into the material of the matter. Might I suggest we would both be more comfortable if we sat down?'

Tully was glad to feel the settee beneath her, but she would have felt much better able to think if Yate had sat anywhere but beside her. Though the settee was not a small one, it appeared so with him sitting so close, his thigh brushing her leg. And if clearing up the fact that she had no interest in Bart, and she still wasn't certain that Yate believed her, wasn't what he wanted to talk to her about, then goodness knew what she was in for now, for her brain appeared to have packed up completely and nothing else was coming through to give her an indication of what was in his mind. Yate was still looking grim, but she didn't swallow his telling her it was because he was unsure of the outcome of their talk. Yate Meachem would always have everything cut and dried. Feeling the silence stretching between them unbearably as she waited for his verbal attack—it could be nothing other than attack, she thought—she just had to say something to try and break the tension.

'At least you're not looking so hostile now as you did when you cut me dead in the hall,' she said, and wished as soon as it was out that she hadn't, he now knew that his freezing glance had got through to her.

'I thought Bart was going to tell me he loved you—that you loved him—that you were going to be married.'

Tully turned to stare at him, her eyes incredulous. He seemed to have forgotten that Bart was in love with Jackie. 'You thought that?' and with further proof that he *had* been thinking that way about her and Bart. 'You wouldn't have liked that, Yate, would you?' she said, and wanted to cry at his low opinion of her as he confirmed roughly,

'I would have hated it like hell.'

There was nothing else she could have said to that if she tried. Tears were threatening to choke her, so she made an unseeing study of her denim-clad knees.

'I don't think,' Yate said slowly, 'I should have been able to take that, Tully Vickery.'

She stood up then. Yate Meachem had had a good go at trampling her pride into the dust but enough was enough. 'Go to hell, Yate Meachem!' she said thickly, and attempting to pull away from his restraining hand, she went to march to the door. In ten minutes she could be away.

The thought was fleeting and perished before it drew breath as no matter how she wrestled to get away from him, his hold on her held fast, and she felt herself being pulled back to the settee. Even her last shreds of dignity vanished as she was pulled down beside him, and to her growing fury found she was anchored down as his arm came over her shoulders and she was forced to sit with his restraining arm about her.

'Whether I go to hell or not we shall see,' he told her gruffly. 'But make no mistake about it, Tully Vickery, neither of us is going anywhere until I've done with you.'

Tully was too defeated to answer him. She had made her attempt to get away, but it hadn't worked. Soon, any second now if her instinct wasn't playing her false, Yate would begin tearing into her about whatever it was that was stewing inside him. All she could hope was that she could gather some remnants of pride from that defeat and hold her end up when the going got rough.

'Now tell me,' said Yate when he had satisfied himself she wasn't going to struggle to get away from his arm, his voice sounding deceptively conversational. 'Tell me just exactly what you were doing in the cashier's office on the night we met?'

CHAPTER ELEVEN

ALARM bells were going off at a terrifying rate in her head. She had thought all that was over and done with, had thought it had been forgotten, never to be mentioned again. But no, here was Yate wanting to go over again what he already knew, and she had a premonition that yet once more she was going to have to fight like the very devil to protect her brother.

'Tell me, Tully,' Yate urged.

'You know what I-I was doing,' she said, trying not to panic. 'You were there—— You saw what I was doing.'

'No,' he said, his very tone telling her he was determined about something. 'I know what I *thought* I saw. Now I'm asking you to tell me what you were *actually* doing.'

She knew she was going to have to lie to him. Well, she was fully prepared to do that. Yate had no time for her, so it wouldn't matter to him. But Richard ... She opened her mouth, ready to continue the lie, turned to Yate to reiterate what she had led him to believe. But, as she looked into his blue eyes, eyes that strangely no longer had that hard glint in them, looked if anything to be saying, trust me, tell me the truth, her voice died and the lies she must utter just wouldn't leave her throat.

'I ...' she tried, but it was no good, she just couldn't lie to him, not even if Richard's life depended on it could she lie to him. She turned her head away hoping her throat would unlock if she wasn't looking at him—but it wouldn't.

What Yate read in her speechless expression she didn't know, but she felt the tightening of his arm about her shoulders. 'Love for a brother is a stronger emotion than we know

175

until it's put to the test.' His voice came quietly, but she had no trouble hearing him as he moved until their two heads were very close.

He must have felt her jerky spasm of movement as the word 'brother' hit her ears. Must have known he was making all the right connections, she thought, willing herself to stay calm, stay cool.

'Can't you tell me, Tully?' Yate asked, and had his answer to that question as her lips stayed firmly closed. If she had been able to say anything at all, it would have been to beg him not to continue to ask what was impossible for her to reveal.

Then when it seemed that minutes had passed and she still hadn't answered him, suddenly, unbelievably, Yate was letting her off the hook. She had known that he rarely said or did what was expected of him, but was astounded when he changed tack completely. She doubted it was because he could see how unhappy his insistence was making her, thought more likely it was because his intelligence was telling him he was getting nowhere on his present course.

'The affection I have for Bart was put severely to the test twelve months ago,' he was saying slowly. 'If you'll bear with me, Tully, I'd like to tell you a little of what led up to it.' And what he had to say next was something that put all thoughts of Richard right out of her head.

'About a year before Bart's accident I decided if there was any chance of this house standing for another couple of hundred years, then regardless of the inconvenience the time had come to put it in order,' he began. 'Out of consideration for my mother who enjoys peace and quiet I had put it off far too long as it was. So after consulting architects, builders and lord knows who else I told Mother and Bart I was going to delay no longer.' Tully began to unwind. She had no idea why Yate was telling her this, but was intrigued nevertheless.

'I'd already found a house where the family and Evie

could move to while the alterations were taking place, then at the last minute when the builders were almost on the doorstep Mother said she couldn't possibly leave, and then Bart said he wasn't going either—Bart manages the estate and was of the opinion that he had to be on hand in case any of the tenants needed to get in touch with him quickly. Much as I didn't want my mother in particular, to put up with the disturbance, but since she was adamant she wasn't going to go, and since the house couldn't be left as it was any longer, there was nothing further I could do.'

Tully felt him looking at her and turned her head to face him. 'Sorry to bore you with all this,' he said, when she wasn't bored at all, 'but it's all leading up to illustrate a point—and perhaps make you see that I'm not the complete blackguard you think I am.' Her heartbeats that had been playing a staccato rhythm hurried up to a faster tempo at that, and she looked away from him.

'To continue,' Yate went on, 'the work had been going on for what seemed like years. I'd been down one weekend, spent the following week in hectic battle fighting off an impudent effort of someone trying their hand at taking over one of the companies I have an interest in, and on the Friday night I decided to come down here again. I arrived late, tired and in need of my bed. What I didn't know,' and here his voice took on a hard edge so that Tully knew he wasn't liking what he had to say next, 'was that Rowena was staying the weekend, didn't know with the bedroom space being scarce since three parts of the house was in one colossal heap, that she had been given the room I'd slept in the previous weekend.'

Tully's heart began playing the Minute Waltz in thirty seconds. She didn't have any trouble recalling that Yate had told her bluntly he had had Rowena in his bed, and suddenly she knew without him telling her that never, ever, would he take advantage of his brother's fiancée. She wanted to tell him so, to get that harsh note out of his voice, but knew she could not. Not without revealing the depth of her feelings for him.

'The room was empty when I went in,' Yate resumed, his voice hard with his remembrances. 'So I went to bed, closed my eyes and would have been asleep within a minute, I swear. Then the next thing I knew was that someone was getting into bed beside me. And then as I went to sit up and put on the bedside lamp, the door opened, the light by the door was switched on and Bart stood there looking as though he'd just received a mule-sized kick in the stomach. I followed his staring, disbelieving eyes, and there, almost purring in bed with me, was Rowena.'

'Oh, Yate,' said Tully, her sympathy all for him, her every feeling tuned to what he must have felt then. 'But you explained what had happened—Rowena . . .'

'I didn't have a chance to say a word, I was too shaken at hearing my brother's fiancée giving her account of how we'd been lovers for some weeks, how she hadn't meant to hurt him but how she hadn't been able to help herself once I'd started to make love to her. Then when I was ready to throw her out of the house neck and crop I looked at Bart and he seemed to be crumbling under the weight of what she was telling him. I knew then that he thought the sun rose and set with that woman. How the hell could I explain anything? He loved her. By thinking me the Judas Rowena was making out I was in seducing her, at least he would keep some of his illusions about her. The rest you know. Bart took off, crashed his car against a brick wall, and once he'd regained consciousness he refused to see me.'

Yate's arm was still around her shoulders, his other hand was resting on his thigh. Tully placed her hand over his, unable to stop herself from wanting to let him know how sorry she was.

'So Bart broke off his engagement?' she asked.

'No, Rowena did that. She was a money-grubbing little bitch. The house had been left to me, but Bart and I had equal shares of Father's money when he died, and while Bart was happy to stay here and manage the estate, I felt the need to have a go at something else—I managed to do quite well,' he added, with masterly understatement, Tully thought. 'I'd noticed Rowena's come-hither glances in my direction before that, but I have been out and about in the world a bit more than Bart, so I had a shrewd idea what she was up to. Anyway, after Bart had rushed out of the house—Mother was asleep while all this was going on, by the way, exhausted probably from the builders' racket— Rowena suggested that the only honourable thing I could do would be to marry her. I left her in no doubt that *that* honourable I wasn't, and she was just letting go, confirming my opinion of her, when the police came to say Bart had had an accident.' Yate turned his hand beneath Tully's, and gripped her hand hard as though the memory was still painful to him. 'As soon as Rowena learned that Bart was going to be in a wheelchair—we didn't know at that time that it wouldn't be permanently—she lit out. I've heard nothing of her since.' Yate came to the end, seemed glad to have done with it, and shifted his position so he could look into Tully's face.

'D-does Bart still believe you—you slept with Rowena?' she asked.

'He did until a couple of hours ago. I wouldn't have told him then when he challenged me about it in the study if he hadn't revealed that only since he had met Jackie, seen the goodness in her, had he begun to see Rowena for what she really was, but said it still stuck in his craw to think I could do such a thing to him. And then, when I was still cogitating if it would have any harmful effect on him to know the truth now that he'd begun to walk again, he told me he no longer believed I'd taken Rowena to bed, regardless of the circumstantial evidence. He'd already told me how you came to be lying on the settee in the drawing room with him. He told me as soon as he realised what I was thinking as I stood there in the doorway, something inside his head clicked, and that unless I told him differently he would never believe it.'

'So you told him?' Tully asked, feeling relief wash over her even before Yate confirmed that Bart now knew Yate's only crime had been in trying to protect him from knowing what sort of a woman he had fallen in love with.

'Yes. As soon as I could see he no longer had any illusions about Rowena, I told him,' Yate said, and smiled briefly. 'Bart called me a few uncomplimentary names I won't offend your ears with, and then he repeated those two words *circumstantial evidence*, reminded me in between expletives that he'd witnessed something twelve months ago that he thought proved every lying word Rowena breathed and that he only saw the truth when I in turn had witnessed something this very morning that looked as though it didn't require words for me to see which way the land lay between the two of you.'

'Oh,' said Tully, feeling her nerves begin to tighten up again. She couldn't think that what Yate had told her was what he had meant to talk about, it couldn't be, because she hadn't seen Bart standing unaided when Yate had expressed a desire to talk to her. She began to feel wary all over again, and knew she had been right to feel so when Yate said:

'Those two words "circumstantial evidence" have been hammering away in my head ever since Bart uttered them.' Yate looked her fully in the face. 'They followed me around all the time I was looking for you. Nobody had seen you, Mother had been outside and said you hadn't passed. I checked your room, you weren't there and though I was sure you wouldn't be up here, I couldn't think where else to look.'

'I . . . I thought I'd come and explain about Bart and me,' she said, feeling she had to say something, might even head him off—well, it was worth a try.

'Circumstantial evidence,' said Yate, his face serious. He

gripped her hand tightly. 'Tully,' he said, then gently, 'dear Tully, please tell me what you were doing in my cashier's office that night?'

'I . . .' Again she couldn't lie to him. She dropped her eyes away from his compelling look so he shouldn't know how his 'dear Tully' had affected her. How deeply she was regretting she couldn't tell him. 'I can't, Yate. Please—please don't ask me.'

She felt his arm tighten again around her as though by her not admitting to guilt he was ready to believe her innocent. Though she couldn't believe that, she felt him give her a small shake, but knew to look at him to try to fathom out what that shake meant would have her going to pieces.

'Tully,' he said her name softly, 'I told you all about that Rowena episode hoping you would see that I'm fully aware of the lengths one will go to in order to save a brother from hurt or trouble.' She tried to pull away, but he refused to release her. 'I *know* Richard is involved somewhere in what you tried to do,' he said clearly. 'You know and I know that he is, and I completely understand your reluctance to tell me seeing that your brother is still in my employ. But I give you my word I won't harm him—won't take his job away from him. Trust me, Tully.'

'Yate.' She looked at him, weakening visibly under the warmth of his look. She did trust him, but even so, the words just wouldn't leave her tongue to denounce Richard. 'Don't make me tell you,' she begged.

She hadn't thought he would listen to her plca, he must know how near to the verge of telling him he had driven her. Then incredulously she heard him saying:

'Perhaps I'm not being fair to you. Perhaps my own need to have you tell me in your own words is blinding me to the fact that wild horses wouldn't drag the confession out of me if it was my brother.' He paused, his eyes steady on hers. 'I remembered something as I was coming to find you, remembered you once saying you were used to tidying up after your brother.' He paused again. 'Tell me, Tully, did Richard take the money?' he asked, when the evidence he had seen was beyond disproving, and then shatteringly, 'Tell me, were you in the act of putting that money back when I interrupted you?'

Tully had to get away from him. She wrenched herself out of his unsuspecting clasp and was at the door before he caught her, caught her and turned her round in his arms.

'I have my answer, haven't I?' he said, and not waiting for her reply, he bent his head and placed his lips against hers.

The magic of his lips seemed what she had been born for. There was no thought of denying him when her arms went up and around him, her response simply the reaction of what he ignited in her. His kiss deepened, his arms pulling her closer to him. She felt the hardness of his thighs and body pressing into her and had no thought to push him away. Her colour was high when Yate broke the kiss, and it was he who relieved the pressure between their two bodies.

'I purposely gave orders that you weren't to sleep in this wing knowing to have you so near would end up in something physical happening between us,' he said, breathing deeply. 'And now you are here, knowing no one will disturb us, I know that I was right.'

Her mind was getting all mixed up again, and much as she wanted him to kiss her again, she knew it must not happen. Yate might desire her, but by what he had just said, he didn't want to give that desire its head. She had to remember she was only here because of the security it had given Bart in his engagement to Jackie. That security was no longer needed now that Bart knew the true situation between Yate and Rowena, and it was painfully obvious that even while Yate desired her, he would loathe himself afterwards, knowing he had taken the sister of someone who had made away with his money—he would probably get round to thinking she was no better than Rowena.

Her arms dropped to her sides. 'I'll go and pack,' she said, pride covering the fact she would probably be in tears before she reached her room. 'I know you only invited me here for Bart's sake—— Well, Bart doesn't need ...'

'Bart's sake be damned!' Yate bit out when she would have turned from him. 'I wanted to see you again—it seemed an eternity since I last saw you. I invited you to come with me because I wanted you with me—Bart's needs had nothing to do with it.'

'You wanted me ...'

'I've wanted you since I saw you asleep on the settee in my apartment,' Yate told her, not sounding very much as though she should believe him. 'You looked so vulnerable, so innocent lying there, your fantastically long eyelashes hiding your beautiful eyes. I wanted to wake you, make you mine, then throw you out for the cheat I thought you were.'

'But you didn't.'

'No—I didn't understand why myself then—as I thought you didn't deserve any better. So I went back to my room fuming against myself for being so weak-kneed. Then even while I was thinking every rotten thing I could about you—how your innocence was no more than skin deep—I found myself collecting a blanket and covering you up in case you were cold.'

Tully remembered the blanket, but something else struck her. Yate had said he didn't understand at the time why he hadn't taken her. She didn't understand why, now, and suddenly it seemed very important that he tell her.

'Why didn't you?' she asked, and went red as she added hesitatingly, 'You said you didn't t-take me and didn't understand why.'

'I thought you would have guessed that by now—I remember telling you I thought you were bright,' he said. 'Why do you think? Why do you think I've had you put in a room so far away from me I'd hoped my ardour would have cooled if I had to go on a route march to get to you?'

'I don't know,' she answered quietly, and felt the rate the blood was speeding through her veins she would faint if he didn't tell her soon.

'Why, because I love you,' Yate said, and was startled when all the colour left her face.

Without wasting time he picked her up in his arms and carried her to the settee to lay her gently down, sitting beside her and not saying another word until the colour began to flood her cheeks again. Tully tried to sit up, only to be pushed gently down again. She just didn't believe what she thought she had heard.

'D-did you say you . . .'

'I love you,' said Yate when she couldn't get the words out.

'But you can't,' she protested, not needing to know now why Yate had wanted her to tell him about Richard as hope roared in; there had to be honesty between them now.

'That's what I thought,' Yate told her. 'I knew you were affecting me in some way, but I put it down to physical chemistry alone. I told myself once I'd taken you to bed . . .' he broke off to kiss her that gentle kiss as she blushed, then leaning back from her went on, 'I thought once we had been lovers I would be free of the pull of you. In less than twenty-four hours you had me irritable, moody—I told myself it was because there was something not very nice about a girl who could try her hand at a little larceny. Then I was shattered when the opportunity presented itself to assuage what I thought was my lust for you, to find I couldn't violate you when I knew you were untouched. Then the next morning I found myself hotly defending you when Bart hinted at breakfast how you came to look so tired. I knew then I loved you—Bart saw it too—and I was as livid as hell. It was all your fault, of course.' Yate smiled engagingly at her. 'I blamed you for making me fall in love with you and was in no mood to be nice to you when we went for a walk. I was hurting like hell, remembering you'd tried to rob me, wanting you to hurt too, remembering Bart's pain —my part in it. I needed to be by myself—I should never have asked you to come with me. Yet when you ran off disgusted at what I'd told you about Rowena and me, I wanted to run after you, to tell you everything that had happened.'

'I had no idea,' Tully said huskily.

'No, I don't suppose you did,' Yate said softly. 'You're particularly innocent where men are concerned, aren't you?' He saw from her face that she was remembering the way she had responded to him that night in the bedroom. 'I know you feel something for me, Tully,' he said, and a frown appeared on his face as he looked at her. 'What do you feel for me? Can you love me, do you think? I'm not always the unpleasant brute I've been to you.'

'You haven't always been unpleasant,' she defended him. 'Sometimes, when you know you've hurt me—you kiss me so gently as though you're saying sorry. I . . .'

'Oh, Tully, you make me feel such a swine that I ever hurt you for a second. Marry me, lovely girl, and I'll make it all up to you.'

'Marry you?' She hadn't meant it to come out sounding so shocked. But she was shocked. Never in her wildest dreams had she thought he would ever ask her to marry him, but she hadn't meant it to sound as if it was the last thing she would think of doing.

Yate was still sitting on the edge of the settee beside her, but she saw his jaw firm before he turned away so she shouldn't see his face and witness his pain.

'Oh God, I've got it all wrong, haven't I?' he breathed. 'I was afraid of this—I've made you hate me.' And before she could break in, 'I knew you weren't in love with Howard, you couldn't have responded to me the way you did if you had been, not you, Tully,' he said as though she was someone very special, someone above cheating on a man. 'I let myself think that since you believed you loved him yet hadn't been to bed with him—since you appeared ready to go to bed with me—then you must be in love with me. It took me a long time to work that out. I wrestled with it all last night—wrestled with myself—and hoped. Hope does funny things to one's thinking,' he said dully, not seeing that she was looking at him with her heart in her eyes. 'I barely slept last night. I wanted to come to you—I almost chased after you when you kissed me at the bottom of the stairs, but forced myself to remember that you had safe-opening tendencies. Then around four o'clock in the morning I knew that, light-fingered or not, it didn't matter.'

'I didn't go to the cashier's office to steal that money.' Tully found her voice. Knowing Yate loved her, would protect her, and Richard if he had to, she confessed openly, 'You were right about the money. I nearly died when I saw it in Richard's briefcase. He wanted it to buy a wine-making business—he should have had one anyway,' she defended him, 'only Monty made some speculations that went dreadfully wrong.'

'I know all that,' Yate told her, staring blankly in front of him. 'Richard wouldn't return the money when he knew you knew about it?'

'No. I nagged him for a solid hour until he finally agreed he'd been very stupid.' She didn't want any secrets between her and Yate now. 'But he wouldn't take it back.'

'Oh, Tully—I daren't look at you for fear I shall ignore your struggles if I obey the impulse to take you in my arms. But oh, my dear, I'd be in heaven if you could love me with half as much of the love you have for your brother.'

'My feelings for you, Yate, are not to be compared with the feelings I have for Richard,' she said quietly, and heard from the anguished breath of pain that Yate had misunderstood her.

'My apologies, Tully,' he said, rising to his feet, his voice deeply controlled. 'It's not like you to be deliberately hurtful, but I can't say in all fairness I didn't deserve that.' He made to move towards the bedroom door, and Tully knew then he would stay inside that room until he was sure she had gone. He wouldn't risk being left alone with her again.

'You misunderstand me,' she said quickly, her voice unconsciously pleading for his understanding before the hardness in him took over. 'The love I have for my brother can in no way be compared with the greater love I have for you—— Please, Yate, let me be your wife.'

Yate turned, the dark frown on his face lifting as he saw her love for him shining from her eyes. In a stride he was back with her, his arms going round her, his mouth kissing hers as though he would never diminish the searing agony her earlier words had burned through him.

'Oh, Tully, my most precious darling, I love you so, I have never felt so dejected in all my life as when I thought I had made you hate me.'

His kisses grew more passionate as her untethered response allowed him anything he might need from her, her own need of him growing as until she knew she would not be the one to draw back, his caressing fingers music to her, blotting out the agonies she had suffered in thinking he wouldn't look twice at her believing what he had of her. But at last, when the bedroom was only a few steps away, Yate sat up, pulling her with him, though he kept his arms tightly about her.

'One more kiss, dearest Tully, and I'm sure I shall blow my mind,' he said thickly, and smiled at her in such a loving way, Tully thought she was in paradise. 'I think perhaps I made the right decision in giving you a room far away from me, sweet temptress—what do you think?' he asked tenderly.

'I . . . I think you might be right,' she answered, having thought he had the power to confuse her before, grateful now to follow his lead in whatever he decided, her own senses seemed to be acting without asking her consent, and lost in Yate's arms she knew her answer would be yes, yes,

yes, had he sought her permission to take her through that bedroom door.

Gently, his voice calming, loving, quiet, Yate brought her down from the fevered pitch of yearning he had taken her to, and though her need of him was recent enough to have her trembling still, she was able to discuss, between his interspersed gentle kisses and endearments, her life at Westover Rise, her work, how soon she could give up her job, and how soon she would marry him.

It was all so unbelievable to be sitting here in the protection of his arms, to find herself being convinced that he meant what he said, that he loved her to distraction, couldn't wait longer than a month to be married to her, and more unbelievable still to find that Yate needed the same assurances from her that she really did love him.

'I feel I ought to pinch myself,' she said after some moments when he had just sat looking at her for the pure joy of it. 'I can't believe this is happening to me—that you really love me.'

'Believe me, my darling,' Yate told her sincerely. 'You have less than a month to get used to the idea, then we'll be married, and if you aren't convinced by then, you'll be in no doubt afterwards.' He kissed her lovingly, and all was quiet for a few minutes before his stronger control had him putting her a little way away from him.

'You'll have to take my word for it until then, sweetheart,' he told her. 'Holding you in my arms is making a nonsense of my thinking.' Tully knew exactly what he meant, his arms affected her more than a little that way themselves. 'I want you to be my wife when I take you to my bed,' Yate told her softly. 'You're so unselfish with those you love, you deserve to be loved in the same way. But believe me, I love you with everything that is in me.'

'I do believe you,' Tully said. She couldn't fail to believe him, not with the love he had for her showing in his face. 'It's just that it's all so unexpected, so new ...'

'I should have told you hours ago,' he said. 'That damned Stuttgart call interrupted everything—— Seeing you in Bart's arms didn't help much either,' he added reminiscently. 'This love feeling is a powerful emotion, Tully—I'd always thought I would do anything for Bart, but when I saw you in his arms this morning I could have killed him without regret. I felt like murder—that's why I had to get out of the house.'

Only then did she gain some idea of how deeply Yate cared for her. He hadn't been joking, she knew, remembering the look that had been on his face. In that moment he had really felt like killing his own brother. Her hand came up to touch his face, wanting him to know she knew how he had felt but how unnecessary that feeling had been. Then something struck her, and her words tumbled over each other as she asked:

'Yate—this morning, when you said you wanted to talk to me—were you going to ask me to marry you then?'

'Yes, of course, I said . . .'

'But you didn't know then that I hadn't been robbing your safe. You didn't know until I . . .'

'I know,' said Yate, mystified why she was so excited but loving the way she was beaming so deliciously at him. 'I told you, darling, I wrestled with myself half the night and knew at four o'clock this morning that only love mattered.'

'You would have married me even had I been the criminal you thought I was?'

Yate began to see then why she was so excited. 'I told you I'm in love with you, Tully,' he said gently. 'Won't you believe me?'

'Oh, Yate,' Tully gasped, tears in her eyes. 'Yes, I do believe you, and I love you so very, very much.'

Harlequin Romances

The books that let you escape
into the wonderful world of romance!
Trips to exotic places … interesting
plots … meeting memorable people …
the excitement of love …. These are
integral parts of Harlequin Romances –
the heartwarming novels read by
women everywhere.

Many early issues are now available.
Choose from this great selection!

Choose from this list of Harlequin Romance editions.*

422 **Then Come Kiss Me**
Mary Burchell

434 **Dear Doctor Everett**
Jean S. MacLeod

459 **Second Love**
(Ring for the Nurse)
Marjorie Moore

481 **Bachelor of Medicine**
Alex Stuart

492 **Follow a Dream**
(Hospital Pro)
Marjorie Moore

508 **Senior Surgeon**
Marjorie Moore

509 **A Year to Remember**
(Nurse Secretary)
Marjorie Moore

517 **Journey in the Sun**
(Doctors Together)
Jean S. MacLeod

535 **Under the Red Cross**
Juliet Shore

559 **The Time of Enchantment**
(Nurse Wayne in the Tropics)
Anne Vinton

583 **This Merry Bond**
Sara Seale

634 **Love without Wings**
(Surgeon's Wife)
Margaret Malcolm

636 **The Home at Hawk's Nest**
(Nurse Candida)
Caroline Trench

673 **Gateway to Happiness**
(Village Clinic)
Ann Cameron

683 **Desire for the Star**
(Doctor's Desire)
Averil Ives

684 **Doctor on Horseback**
Alex Stuart

713 **Harvest of the Heart**
(Nurse of My Heart)
Jill Christian

714 **Conduct Unbecoming**
(Young Nurse Payne)
Valerie K. Nelson

729 **One with the Wind**
(Surgeons at Arms)
Mary Hunton

737 **Maiden Flight**
Betty Beaty

746 **Loyal in All**
(Nurse Marika, Loyal in All)
Mary Burchell

748 **The Valley of Palms**
Jean S. MacLeod

798 **If This Is Love**
Anne Weale

799 **Love Is for Ever**
Barbara Rowan

810 **The Piper of Laide**
(Doctor of Rhua)
Alex Stuart

815 **Young Tracy**
Rosalind Brett

838 **Dear Dragon**
Sara Seale

872 **Haven of the Heart**
Averil Ives

878 **The Dangerous Kind of Love**
(This Kind of Love)
Kathryn Blair

888 **Heart of a Rose**
Rachel Lindsay

902 **Mountain of Dreams**
Barbara Rowen

903 **So Loved and So Far**
Elizabeth Hoy

909 **Desert Doorway**
Pamela Kent

920 **The Man at Mulera**
Kathryn Blair

927 **The Scars Shall Fade**
Nerina Hilliard

941 **Mayenga Farm**
Kathryn Blair

Some of these book were originally published under different titles.